A
Li

n

NIMBUS
PUBLISHING LTD
nimbus.ca

Nimbus Publishing Limited
3731 Mackintosh St, Halifax, NS, B3K 5A5
(902) 455-4286 nimbus.ca

This novel is a work of fiction. Names, characters, places, and incidents are either the product of the author's imagination or are used fictitiously.

Printed and bound in Canada
Cover Design: Sari Naworynski
Interior Design: Meredith Bangay
Cover photos: (newspaper clipping) Nova Scotia Archives; (children) stock; (clock and explosion cloud) Maritime Museum of the Atlantic

NB1302
Library and Archives Canada Cataloguing in Publication

Lawson, Julie, 1947-, author
A blinding light / Julie Lawson.
ISBN 978-1-77108-541-0 (softcover)
1. Halifax Explosion, Halifax, N.S., 1917—Juvenile fiction. I. Title.

PS8573.A94B55 2017 jC813'.54 C2017-904111-8

Nimbus Publishing acknowledges the financial support for its publishing activities from the Government of Canada through the Canada Book Fund (CBF) and the Canada Council for the Arts, and from the Province of Nova Scotia. We are pleased to work in partnership with the Province of Nova Scotia to develop and promote our creative industries for the benefit of all Nova Scotians.

For my great-niece Piper,
future keeper of the family stories,
whose great-great-Grandpa Goodwin was
in Halifax on December 6, 1917

CHAPTER 1

Saturday, November 10, 1917

The sailboat, *Seevögel*, lived up to her name, skimming over the waves like a seabird. Flying, flying, the skipper laughing in the face of a stinging wind—until the unthinkable happened.

The mast snapped.

Seevögel collapsed in a crumpled heap of sails, dragged under by the weight of water.

The skipper would have been lost at sea if he hadn't managed to swim ashore, determined to make his way home. That's how Livy saw it. No matter how often she was told otherwise, she believed that her father was alive. Even though he'd been gone a long time. Not three years gone, like the soldiers who were off fighting in the Great War, but still. Six months was a long time to be waiting.

She tightened the scarf around her neck and picked up her pace. Now that she'd come out of the wooded section of Point Pleasant Park and was on the beach, there was no escaping the bite of the wind. How stupid she'd been to forget her hat! She could already hear her mother scolding. *That'll teach you, Olivia. Being in such an all-fired hurry to leave the house….*

Her ears were numb and the wind was running wild with her hair. The curls would be a tangled mess by the time she got home, and there'd be more grumbling and scolding about that, but Livy didn't care. The sun was shining and it was good to be outside. And if she wore her scarf over her ears instead of around her neck, the cold ear problem would be solved.

She made the switch, tied the scarf ends under her chin, and ran to the point where the waters divided. The Northwest Arm on the west, Halifax Harbour on the east. Nothing was moving on the Arm, but a ship was just now steaming up the harbour past McNabs Island. She'd sail up between Halifax and Dartmouth, through the Narrows, and into Bedford Basin to be moored.

Livy's dad had loved coming here. So had her brother, Will. They'd watch the ships coming and going, but unlike Livy, they'd know something about them. They'd talk endlessly about where the ships were heading, where they were from, what they were carrying, what life might be like on board. The times they let her tag along, she'd join in too, feigning an interest. She'd put up with anything to be included—the cold, the hours of standing, the nautical terms she didn't understand. Any kind of ship drew their attention. But for Livy, the only one that mattered was *Seevögel*, Dad's beloved sailboat.

Her hair blew across her face and her heart lurched. *He* never scolded or minded that her hair was in tangles....

"Livy! Didn't think I'd find you here."

The high-pitched voice yanked her back to the present. *Lewis Fraser.* She groaned. Thin and gangly, with a freckled face and sandy-coloured hair even more unruly than her own, he was the most annoying person in the world and the last person she *ever* wanted to see.

"Don't lie, Lewis. You knew I was here because you followed me. Didn't you?" For the last four months, since the Dominion Day party at the church, he'd been trying to get her attention. "Well?" she prodded. "Didn't you?"

He ignored the question and pointed out that her scarf was slipping off her head. "Do you want to wear my hat? It'll keep your ears warm."

"And get your cooties? I'm not that desperate."

"Your scarf's not long enough to tie properly."

She readjusted her scarf to prove him wrong.

"Are you coming here tomorrow?" he said.

"Tomorrow's Stir-up Sunday so we're making the Christmas pudding—as you well know, since you do the same thing at your house every year. And if I *was* coming here, you'd be the last person to know."

"Sure you don't want my hat?" He took it off and held it out to her.

"It's full of cooties!" She slapped it away. "I'm warning you, Lewis, if you don't stop bothering me I'm going to tell Will. Then you'll be sorry."

He nodded and looked serious for all of one second. Then he grinned—the most irritating, lopsided, stupid, dimply grin—and said, "You want to go somewhere?"

"*No!* And we *are* somewhere. It's where I wanted to be and I wanted to be here alone. Now you've come and spoiled everything." She spun around and headed towards the path in the woods.

He was right at her heels.

"Get lost!" she yelled over her shoulder.

"Wait! I've got something important to tell you."

"No, you don't! You never do! You're worse than a puppy!" Before long, Livy had left Lewis behind and dismissed him from her mind.

Her earlier thoughts weren't as easy to dismiss. They stayed with her during the expected scolding from her mother—a scolding that, for once, she endured in silence. And they were still on her mind that evening, taking her back to the last day she'd spent with her father.

Saturday, May 12, 1917

It was a day Livy had looked forward to. A *whole* day of sailing, not just a couple of hours. Dad had even asked

Hannah to pack them a picnic. She'd complained, but no one had paid any attention. As the live-in cook and housekeeper who'd been with the family forever—even during Livy's grandparents' time—she was entitled to a few complaints.

The plan was to stop at one of the small islands or, if the day was especially fine, sail the whole length of the Northwest Arm and out into the harbour as far as McNabs Cove.

"But we won't go past McNabs Island," Livy said, wanting reassurance that they wouldn't venture into the Atlantic—not with German submarines prowling the area.

"Don't worry," said Dad, "we'll be safe as houses."

They loaded the picnic hamper into their new motorcar, waved goodbye to Mum and Hannah, and were soon on the road. The small marina where Dad moored *Seevögel* wasn't far, but walking would mean less time for sailing. And taking the car gave Will an opportunity to practise his driving, since he was almost old enough to apply for his license.

"Well done," Dad said after Will had expertly parked the car. "You two run on ahead. I'll bring the picnic basket."

"Race you, Will!" Livy sprinted off, laughing, before her brother had a chance to reply.

"Cheater! You had a head start!"

Livy had almost reached the sailboat when she stopped short, her laughter caught in her throat. Someone had crossed out the name *Seevögel* and, in huge red letters, painted the words KILLER KRAUT.

Will, and their father soon after, joined her in shocked silence. From past experience, they knew there was no point in reporting the damage. They'd never find out who'd done it. And there was no point in asking why. They knew the answer.

Livy's eyes welled up with tears. "What should we do now?"

"Paint over it like before," Dad said. He gave a resigned sigh. "We'll go sailing tomorrow."

"Maybe we shouldn't call it *Seevögel* this time," said Will. "Use the English name, *Seabird*."

"It's bad luck to change the name of a boat," Dad said.

"Well *Seevögel* hasn't exactly brought us good luck," Will muttered.

"And *Seabird* isn't a change," Livy added. "It's a translation."

"You've got a point," said Dad. "Let me think about it." He left them with instructions to sand off the words while he drove to town to buy paint.

For a long time they worked in silence. Then Will burst out, "What did he expect? He knows how people feel about the Germans. This is the third time the sailboat's been vandalized. He should have changed the name as soon as the war started."

"It's only a word," Livy said, though she knew Will was right. Dad couldn't change his German name or his accent, but he didn't have to draw attention to it. She hated the way he'd talk to her friends if they happened to meet in town or on the street. Couldn't he just *nod* a hello? Or ignore them? Did he have to *talk*? She'd seen the girls snicker as they walked away. Bystanders, too—only they were more likely to scowl. It wasn't fair to *her*. She rubbed the sandpaper in angry circles as flecks of red enamel paint drifted down to the water.

"At least it's warm and sunny," Dad said when he returned. "The paint will dry in no time, and we can row out in the dory between coats. We won't be able to go as far but we can still have our picnic."

"What about the name?" Will asked. "Have you decided?"

"For the time being we'll leave her nameless. Is that a good idea?"

Will nodded, visibly relieved.

• • •

The next day had been cold and windy. "I hate to disappoint you," Dad said at breakfast, "but it's best if I go out on my own today. Look at that sky. It's going to rain for sure."

"We don't care," said Will. "Come on, Dad."

"You promised," Livy added. "We don't mind the wind, and it's not raining yet."

"So says my fair-weather sailor." Dad grinned, and chucked her under the chin. "You're the one who begs to go home at the first sign of a whitecap. You panic when I lean out over the side."

"I do not! Only that one time."

"*Every* time, Livy," Will said. "I'll come with you, Dad. I love leaning out in the wind. Last time you said I was a big help. You said—"

"Don't even think about it." Their mother had joined them at the table. "No arguing," she said sternly. "You two are staying put."

"I'm almost sixteen!" Will protested. "It's not like there's going to be a hurricane."

Mum went on as if she hadn't heard. "As for you, Ernst Schneider, you're a daft fool if you go out today. It's blowing up for a storm."

"Perfect for sailing, Fiona. Especially if you're as daft as I am." He poured himself another cup of coffee. "Now that that's settled, let's enjoy the rest of our breakfast."

He'd left a short time later.

Livy remembered watching him drive away. He'd looked up at the house and she'd waved from her bedroom window. Had he seen her? She hoped so, though he hadn't waved back. It saddened her to think that she'd left the breakfast table in a sulk, and without saying goodbye.

That night, Livy had been awakened by the sound of a motorcar stopping in front of her house. She'd leapt out of bed, assuming that it was her father. They hadn't worried when he hadn't come home by dinner, because he often met friends at the marina after a day's sail and lost track of time. It was unusual, though, for him to be gone this long after dark. *He'll get some scolding from Mum*, Livy thought. She opened the curtains to look outside and drew back in alarm. It was a police car, not Dad's motorcar. Two policemen were approaching the front door.

Why?

The possibilities ran through her head. *They've come to arrest him. They'll put him in a camp with the enemy aliens, that's what they'll call him. Only he's not an alien, he's a Canadian, and he's not an enemy. They don't know he's not home....*

What if they've come to tell us he's already been arrested? What if he sailed to Melville Island where the German prisoners of war are being kept and he was caught trying to talk to one of them? Was that his plan all along? Was that why he wanted to go sailing by himself?

Stop it, Livy! How could she think that way? Dad would never do such a thing. The rumours were getting to her. Just because a person was from Germany didn't make him a spy.

*But what if...*her mind stirred up yet another possibility. *What if he somehow found out that he was about to be arrested? Is that why he hasn't come home? He didn't want to embarrass us, so he's hiding somewhere?* On and on her thoughts went, racing as wildly as her heartbeat.

When she heard a knock on the door, she left her room and crept down the hall to the top of the stairs.

"Come in, officers," her mother was saying.

The men stepped inside and closed the door behind them. "We're sorry, Mrs. Schneider," one officer began. "Is there somewhere we could sit?"

"Of course," Mum said. "The parlour's this way."

"What's happened?" Livy heard Will say. She wasn't surprised that her brother was still up. He often stayed up late to play chess with Mum, whether Dad was home or not.

It was difficult to make out what the policemen were saying, now that they'd gone into the parlour. Whatever it was, Livy could tell from their tone that it was a serious matter. She went down a few stairs and strained to listen.

"Are you sure?" Will said.

"Yes...possible drowning...search party tomorrow... doesn't look hopeful."

"Doesn't look hopeful?" Mum's voice was clear. "You don't say that until you find the body. Until then, there's hope. Do you understand?"

Livy couldn't see her, but she knew Mum's mouth would be set in a thin line, her eyes would be hard, and she would be standing straight and tall, the way she did when she found herself in a difficult situation (seldom) or when she wanted to be in control (always).

"Of course, ma'am. We'll keep you informed. And tomorrow, we'll need you to come to the station. There's the matter of your motorcar."

"Can I help with the search tomorrow?" Will said.

"No!" Mum said sharply. "You let them do their job, Will. It's not something you want to be involved in, in case—I'm sorry. Good night, officers. If you'll excuse me...."

After Will had seen the officers out, Livy heard her mother say, "An accident. That's all you need to tell Olivia or anyone else who asks. An accident."

"Mum, you're not thinking straight. Of course it was an accident. What else would it be?"

She was silent for a moment, as if weighing the possible answers to his question. Then she ended the matter by saying, "Quite right, Will. An accident. Leave the chessboard as it is. We'll continue tomorrow."

With that she'd gone upstairs to her room, walking past Livy without saying a word.

As if I wasn't there, Livy remembered. *As if I was invisible.*

• • •

The search for Ernst Schneider had ended after three days. No trace of him was found. It was assumed he had drowned or been hit by a falling mast, and his body washed out to sea.

Livy blamed herself and Will. They should have let Dad repaint the name *Seevögel*. He'd known it was bad luck to change the name. Maybe it was even worse luck to leave a boat without one. He'd given in to what they'd wanted. It was their fault.

His damaged sailboat had been towed back to the marina and her broken mast replaced. Six months later, she was still there and still nameless. Waiting, like Livy, for the skipper's return.

CHAPTER 2

Monday, November 26, 1917

For once Livy had the whole house to herself. Mum was somewhere in the North End doing good deeds and Will had left for school, probably by way of the harbour to watch the ships. Hannah was shopping at the Public Market and the servant girl, Kathleen, was in some far corner of the house doing whatever housework she did on a Monday morning. With no one around to care what Livy did or didn't do, she finished her cereal and headed for the front parlour.

The large, sunny room with its rounded bay windows was Livy's favourite room in the house. It was strictly reserved for company and special occasions, but for the next thirty minutes, it was all hers. She could put a record on the gramophone and waltz around the furniture, or conduct an imaginary orchestra. She could play the piano as loudly and imperfectly as she liked without Mum yelling at her to stop. She could pick up and examine the items that had once belonged to her grandparents and great-grandparents, items that were too valuable for children (even twelve-year-olds) to *look* at, let alone touch.

The first thing to do was to tie back the floor-to-ceiling curtains and let in the light. Once that was done, she took on the role of Olivia, Acclaimed Pianist, standing in the spotlight of the morning sun to thunderous applause.

She bowed to her invisible audience, feeling proud but a little nervous. As if she really *was* performing in a concert hall. In her mind's eye she searched the crowd for familiar faces. Most were difficult to make out in the glare of the spotlight, but she did manage to spot her father. After blowing him a kiss, she addressed the audience. "Thank you for coming. I shall now play a famous minuet by Mozart."

She adjusted the piano stool and sat down to play. Her hands danced over the keys, not a wrong note anywhere. She paused at the end to let the final chord linger, then stood to take her bows.

Oh, the applause! The shouts of *Encore*! She twirled around the room, curtseying, blowing kisses, flinging out her arms as if to embrace her fans—and knocked a priceless crystal vase off the sideboard.

"Oh, no!" She clapped her hand to her mouth, her heart thumping against her ribs. The vase was shattered.

Worse, it wasn't just *any* vase. Of all the objects in the room, it was Mum's favourite. Livy's too. Even as a baby she'd been drawn to it, the way it sparkled and reflected the light, the way it made rainbows shimmer on the walls and floor. She remembered how she'd pretend to catch the rainbows and hand them to her father. How he'd pick her up to examine the prisms, being careful that her small, often sticky fingers never touched the vase.

She forced herself to look down at the hardwood floor, at the splinters of glass that had once taken the shape of a family heirloom. If only it had fallen on the carpet. The thickness might have cushioned the blow and the vase might have stayed in one piece. But it hadn't. And now it was a right holy mess.

What to do? Only one choice, really. To make like it never happened.

She put the room back to the way she'd found it. Untied the curtains. Closed the lid on the piano. Set the stool back in place. Left the room and shut the door behind her.

Then she went into the hall, put on her coat, picked up her school satchel, and left the house. She hadn't gone far when something made her look back. And there was Kathleen, watching her from the turret window, her face creased in a frown.

She must have heard everything. The piano, the crash, and when Mum gets home....

But then again, maybe not. Kathleen could have been in another part of the house at the time, working away and singing—Kathleen was always singing, in spite of Mum's disapproval—and she might *not* have heard.

As Livy continued down the street, she began to rehearse what she'd say if an apology were needed. *It was an accident, Mum. I'm sorry....*

But was she? As horrible as it sounded, Livy had to admit she wasn't sorry. She wished it hadn't been that particular vase, but other than that? She wasn't one bit sorry. She wished she'd smashed a dozen vases to show Mum how broken *she'd* been feeling since Dad had gone. Unless it was to scold or criticize, Mum took no notice of Livy whatsoever. She might as well have gone away too.

By the time Livy reached the corner, Eliza was stomping with impatience. "What took you so long? I have to tell you, I was at the Red Cross the other day—the meeting you couldn't go to, remember? And we were rolling bandages and some of the girls got to talking and Beth was saying that her mother knows your mother because of the Temperance Society, and they were at a meeting and Beth's mother...."

By now, Livy had done what she usually did with Eliza. She'd tuned her out to think about other things. Like that Lewis. How could she get him to stop pestering her? Nothing she did or said made a difference. Did he actually *like* being told to get lost, time after time? As for the Junior Red Cross, she couldn't miss another meeting, and she was way behind on the balaclavas she'd promised to knit for the soldiers fighting in France—"Stop!" she said suddenly, picking up on a part of Eliza's chatter. "What did you just say?"

"About the Temperance Society?"

"No, after that. Just now. About my dad."

"Oh, that. It probably isn't true, but Beth's mother said that he was accused of sabotage. You know, when that bridge was blown up?"

"That was years ago! And Dad was never accused of blowing up a bridge. Why are you bringing that up?"

"Because Beth's mother said that she knows someone and *he* said that your dad was going to be arrested. But then he went sailing and, well, you know. Don't look at me like that! You know it isn't true and anyway it doesn't matter, does it? Because he never got arrested."

"Because he died! I suppose you think that's better than being arrested." *Except that he didn't die.* But Livy wasn't about to share her secret belief with Eliza.

"Come on," Eliza said, linking her arm through Livy's. "You know I didn't mean it that way."

Livy tore her arm away. "How *did* you mean it? Some friend! How can you be so hurtful?" Choking back tears, she stomped on ahead.

Her dad, a spy? Ridiculous! And yet, when the police had come that night, how quickly the possibility had sprung into her mind. Even now, she felt ashamed.

Of course he wasn't a spy. He had a German name but he was a Canadian citizen. He'd lived in Halifax for years and worked as an accountant. No one was a better Canadian. Just because he hadn't joined up to fight in France—he'd wanted to! It wasn't his fault the army had rejected him for being too old.

Trust Eliza to bring up something that no longer mattered. She'd always taken Livy's side when some of the girls at school taunted her for being half-German, or mocked her by speaking in a German accent—*"Hi, Livyvurst! Vat do you vant to do this morninka?"*—but behind her back? Eliza was probably the same as the others. Everyone blamed the Germans for starting the war, and it was true. But the Germans who lived in Halifax, on the other side of the Atlantic, in North America for heaven's sake, what did they have to do with it? Easy targets, that's all they were. Someone to blame when the never-ending lists of dead and injured soldiers appeared in the newspapers.

Not that blaming did any good. The soldiers were still dead. The war was still on. Dad was still out there, somewhere.

CHAPTER 3

Friday, November 30, 1917

Will never went directly to school. His routine was to leave the house early and walk up Citadel Hill for a view of the harbour or, as on this particular morning, walk down to the harbour itself. There was always something going on and someone to talk to about the movement of the various ships. Now that he was the editor of his school's newspaper and wrote a regular editorial on shipping news, it was important that he keep up-to-date reports.

As luck would have it, he spotted a familiar figure a few yards ahead. The portly man with the mustache was Captain Mackey, one of the local pilots who guided vessels in and out of the harbour. His shifts were always changing, but since he didn't live far from Will their paths sometimes crossed.

"Captain Mackey!" Will called, and ran to catch up. "Mind if I walk with you?"

"'Course not, Will," the pilot said, turning to greet him. "Where're you off to? Let me guess. You've got your notebook handy and you're going to check on what's what at the harbour."

"You know me!" Will laughed.

"I reckon I know a future pilot." Captain Mackey winked and eyed Will thoughtfully. "How much longer have you got? It can't be too long."

"Two more years of school," Will said. "Then I'll do whatever it takes to get my pilot's license."

"It's not an easy job, you know," the pilot said. "Storms like you wouldn't believe. A couple of times, the storms were so fierce I couldn't get off the ship I was piloting. Once I ended up going to New York. Second time, I went all the way to England. My kids were some tickled when I came home with presents."

Will smiled. "The hardest part of your job must be boarding the other vessel. Wouldn't you say so? Climbing up and down those rope ladders must take some courage."

"Sure does," Captain Mackey said. "If a hand or a foot slips, you're either in the water or you're bashing yourself on the pilot boat idling below. Oh, it's tough, all right. Especially in cold weather."

"Is it true you can't wear mittens, even when it's below freezing?"

"True enough, and that's because the wool sticks to the rope. So you climb with bare hands. It doesn't take long before your fingers go numb and you can't grip the ladder. So you don't dawdle when you're climbing up or down. Oh, it's dangerous work. But I wouldn't trade jobs if you paid me."

Will grinned. That was the life for him. Danger meant adventure.

They walked along, chatting about marine matters, until Captain Mackey said, "I'll be turning off here, Will. Always nice to see you. Any time you want information for your shipping news column, or if you have a question about piloting, let me know. We need eager young fellows like you."

"Thanks, Captain," Will said, and gave him a friendly wave.

He hadn't gone much farther when he ran into a former schoolmate, Edward Beazley. "On your way to work?" Will asked. He couldn't help but feel jealous. At fifteen, Edward was already working as a clerk in the pilotage office.

"Yup, it's off to work for me," Edward said. "You know the worst thing about my job?"

Will couldn't imagine.

"It's calling over to the *Niobe.* You know, the ship where the Canadian Navy has its headquarters?"

Will said nothing. Of course he knew about the *Niobe*. He also knew that Edward liked to give the impression of knowing more than mere schoolboys like Will, even if they were the same age.

"It's that Wyatt," Edward said. "You know, the chief examining officer? He came up with a new rule last May. Says that the pilots have to call his office whenever there's a ship going out on its own. You know, not part of a convoy. What a headache! Pilots don't like it one bit, I can tell you."

Will had heard about the rule from Captain Mackey but decided to let Edward be the know-it-all. Besides, once Edward got started, he was almost impossible to stop.

"Pilots said it was a waste of time. You know, making the call and waiting around for Wyatt to come to the phone. So they asked me to handle it. Well, if Wyatt or some assistant answered the phone, fine and dandy. I knew they were listening, 'cause when I reeled off the names, they'd sometimes tell me to slow down, or they'd ask me to repeat a name or spell it, you know, so they could write it down correctly. Sometimes there'd be more than a dozen names. It wasn't an easy task and you know how fast I talk sometimes."

All the time, thought Will. "So what was the problem?"

"The clerks in Wyatt's office! A bunch of arrogant you-know-whats, and they didn't listen to a word I said. Didn't ask a single question about names or times of departures—nope, just stayed silent, even when I deliberately talked faster. I knew they weren't writing down the names. Nobody could write *that* fast. And a couple of times—get this—I could hear the other clerks laughing in the background. Laughing! Like I was some kind of a joke."

Edward had always boasted about his job and how important it was. For him to admit that he felt like a joke was something. Will made some appropriate sounds of understanding.

"Oh, it doesn't matter now," Edward said with a laugh. "I just stopped calling. The pilots know what they're doing, so there's no need to worry. Well, here's where I leave you, Will. See you around."

Will waved and carried on to the waterfront.

Even as a young boy, Will had been drawn to the harbour. Most mornings he'd go down with his dad. They'd watch the ships until it was time for Dad to head to his office and Will to get to school. Early on, he'd followed Dad's practice of keeping a notebook to record the marine traffic. He'd started it as a hobby, never dreaming that his country would one day be part of the Great War, and that the ships passing in and out of his city would have an impact on lives far away from Canadian shores.

There were so many ships! In the last month alone Will had seen troop ships loaded with soldiers destined for France, and supply ships taking wheat, horses, and other essentials overseas to the fighting troops. He'd seen relief ships from neutral countries like Norway carrying food to the starving people in Belgium. The small ferryboats that carried passengers between Halifax and Dartmouth were a daily occurrence, as were tugs, barges, and pilot boats. There were hospital ships, cruisers, freighters, and, most impressive of all, massive British destroyers that led ships across the Atlantic in convoys. It was the only way to protect the ships from German submarines.

Will couldn't remember when he'd first noticed how wistfully his dad used to gaze at the outgoing ships. Once, Dad had told him to follow his own dreams, not some plan laid out by others. *It never works, Will*, he'd said. *You end up spending a life of "could haves" and "should haves."*

Not me, Will had thought. Without being told, he knew that his dad would rather have been a sailor than an accountant. He'd loved the sea. He'd loved talking to ordinary sailors, and was a friend of many of the local captains and pilots. Some of Will's happiest moments had been spent with his dad on the docks, listening to Captain Mackey tell of his adventures.

Thinking of Captain Mackey turned Will's attention to a pilot boat just setting out. *That* was his dream. Sure, it was dangerous work. Halifax Harbour itself was dangerous. Not only was there the weather to worry about—fog could appear in seconds—there were strong currents, rocks, and shoals. Not to mention the tides that could work for or against a ship. The very shape of the harbour made things difficult. It was like an hourglass, with the Bedford Basin at one end, the outer harbour at the other, and a narrow pinched-in part in between. That part, "the Narrows," was where a pilot could really show his mettle. Because once a ship entered a harbour, the pilot was in charge, not the ship's captain.

Will looked out at the harbour and smiled, picturing his future self as a pilot ruling those waters. He'd wear a uniform and be so important that Kathleen would be sure to take notice, even though she was two years older. There'd be no more teasing him about being a schoolboy.

"What are you grinning about?" Will's best friend, Henry, shouted up from the dock.

Will blushed, embarrassed at having been caught daydreaming. The last thing he wanted was for Henry to find out he had a crush on his family's servant girl. "Got an earful from Edward this morning," he said hurriedly, and related the conversation.

"So Edward just went ahead and stopped calling Wyatt's office? Even though he was supposed to?" Henry laughed. "Gosh. You don't want to treat him as a joke."

"I hope he doesn't get fired for disobeying orders," said Will.

"Liar!" Henry gave him a playful punch on the arm. "You'd be down there in a second applying for his job. Hey, I've been wondering. You ever think you'd want to be a spy?"

"Don't start that again."

"I don't mean like your dad. I mean, spying for our side. You could lie about your age and join up—you look old enough—and spy on the Germans. You speak German, don't you?"

Will struggled to control his temper. "Three things. First, I don't speak German. Second, I know of men shooting themselves in the foot to avoid going overseas. Third, for the hundredth time, my dad wasn't a spy."

"It's just that—well, some of the boys were telling me that your dad was going to be arrested—"

"Don't start!" Will pushed Henry, harder than he'd intended to, causing him to fall back against a coil of rope.

"What's with you?" Henry said. "I was only kidding, for crying out loud. I could've landed in the water."

"You started it," Will shot back. "I warned you, didn't I? It's not like it's the first time. You're some stupid, you are."

"All right, take it easy." Henry heaved a sigh and got to his feet. He held out his hand. "Still pals?"

"You don't deserve it." Will reluctantly shook Henry's hand. "My dad's gone. Why can't you just let it go? Why can't *they*? It's been months. *Years*."

Two years since a German saboteur had blown up a bridge between the U.S. and New Brunswick. Months since another saboteur had caused a munitions plant in New Jersey to go up in flames. An accident, as it turned out, but the damage was done. Germans, even if they were Canadian citizens, were eyed with suspicion.

In the early years of the war, Will had often lashed out at schoolmates for taunting him. Chief amongst them was Percy George, a bully who had picked on Will as early as the first grade. Henry and a few other friends had been occasional victims, but since the start of the war Percy had focused on Will—making fun of his given name, *Wilhelm*, referring to his dad as *Fritz* or *Kraut*, accusing him of being a spy. Will suspected that Percy was behind the broken windows in his dad's office, as well as the graffiti on his sailboat.

Will had fought back at the beginning. His fights in defense of his dad had gotten him strapped at school more times than he could remember, and once, he'd been suspended. Mum had been furious. Dad, quietly disapproving. "I'm sorry you have to go through this," he'd said. "But I don't need you to fight my battles. Let it be. Sooner or later the war will be over and things will settle down."

Will had taken his dad's advice—bitten his tongue, held his fists, and walked away from confrontations. Since the boating accident, Percy seemed to have given up on him. It wasn't as much fun if your target couldn't be provoked. Or maybe Percy had outgrown his bullying stage.

Will thought he'd outgrown his fighting-back stage but clearly, he hadn't. "I'm sorry, Henry," he said after a while. "I get so fed up sometimes. I didn't mean to lose my temper."

"Forget it," said Henry. "I shouldn't have rattled you. It's just that…we got a telegram yesterday. Remember my cousin Jack, the one who used to take us fishing? He got killed at Passchendaele."

Will knew that Jack was Henry's favourite cousin. "Oh, gosh, Henry. I'm so sorry. If there's anything I can do…."

"Thanks, pal." He gave a loud sigh. "I'm going to school now. Coming?"

Will shook his head. "I'll stay a bit longer. There's a ship coming in." He jotted down a few notes on ship traffic but found it difficult to concentrate, given the news of Henry's loss and the persistent rumours surrounding his father.

When would they end? Since the war started there'd been rumours about his dad being a spy. Will didn't believe it, but he had to wonder. The way Dad had talked to sailors on the docks, his interest in ships—when they were leaving, where they were going, what they were carrying. The times he'd gone away on business. Or so he'd said. Business that sometimes took him to Amherst, where many Germans had been interned. Will didn't want to upset Livy by asking if she'd ever wondered about such things, and he wouldn't dare bring it up with his mother. Could the rumours have been true?

Absolutely not. He refused to let them spoil another minute of the day.

But the damage had been done. That's the way it was with rumours. They aroused suspicion. Made you unwary. Made you think, if only for a minute, that the impossible could in fact be true.

CHAPTER 4

Wednesday, December 5, 1917

Livy had never seen her mother in such a state. Twelve ladies from the Halifax Red Cross were coming that afternoon for their weekly meeting and she had no help. No one to clean the house (already spotless) or polish the silver (gleaming). No one to set out the good china or serve the tea that was as essential to a meeting as the business agenda. No one to clear the table or do the washing up afterwards.

"I've had no time to interview anyone," she said. "No time to find someone suitable, and I can't expect Hannah to do everything, not at her age. Honestly, I never would have thought that of Kathleen. Almost two years she's been working here, and never a problem. Never. I had doubts when I hired her, seeing as how she was only fifteen, but up until now she's been beyond reproach, the best servant we've ever had. Trustworthy, polite, respectful, intelligent—how could she have been so careless? And my favourite vase—oh, you can't imagine!"

"Let me help," Livy said. For the first time in ages, her mum was talking to her. *Ranting* was more like it, but at least it was some kind of notice. Seizing the opportunity, she took the lace tablecloth from her mother's hands and laid it on the table. "Cups and saucers next?"

"Not until you've straightened the cloth. And don't carry so much at a time, you'll drop something." She paused for a breath, but couldn't stay silent for long. "Oh, for goodness sake, Olivia. Do I have to watch your every move? You're getting fingerprints all over the spoons."

"I'm trying to be helpful!" Livy burst out. "You don't have to supervise *for goodness sake*!"

"Enough of the sass, my girl." She gave Livy a warning look and headed off to the kitchen to check on Hannah's tea cakes.

Livy held her tongue and continued to set the table. Cups, saucers, teaspoons, cake plates, sugar bowl, cream jug, linen napkins—everything in its proper place, the way she'd seen it a hundred times before. There. She stepped back, proudly surveying her work.

"Not those napkins!" Mum's voice came from over her shoulder. "We use the embroidered napkins for company. Haven't I taught you anything?"

Crushed by the criticism, Livy retorted, "Not this sort of thing! We've always had servants. I can't do *housework*."

"It's time you learned. Maybe it's a good thing Kathleen's gone. Maybe I won't bother finding a replacement. Would that make you happy, doing a servant's job? Maybe you could learn to dust a vase without smashing it to pieces. And stop picking the fluff off your sweater!" She gave Livy's hand a smack. "How many times have I told you? You'll get bits of wool on the china!" She handed Livy the for-company napkins. "Here. Put the other ones back in the drawer. And when you've done that, go upstairs and tie back your hair. I can't bear to see it flopping in front of your face like that. I should've made you wear a cap, like Kathleen—"

"She didn't break the vase." The words came out as if they had a mind of their own. "It was me. I did it."

Her mother gaped, for once at a loss for words.

"I tried to tell you," Livy continued. A lie, but Mum wasn't to know. "You wouldn't listen. You *never* listen to me. You assumed it was Kathleen and dismissed her on the spot."

"You dreadful girl!" Mum grabbed her by the shoulders and shook her. "You let Kathleen take the blame? How could you be so deceitful?"

"I wasn't thinking. I'm sorry."

"*Sorry*? You're going to be a lot sorrier, young lady. You don't know the meaning of the word. Go to your room. We'll talk about this later."

Livy went upstairs, her shoulders aching from her mum's sharp fingernails. She'd be punished, no doubt about that. She'd be confined to her room for a week (except to go to school), and she'd lose her pocket money. She might even get her knuckles rapped. Nothing that she didn't deserve.

She sat at her window and watched the ladies arrive. Her bedroom was above the dining room, and it wasn't long before the room was filled with the sound of their voices. If Mum wasn't hosting or attending one meeting, it was another. Today it was the Halifax Red Cross. Another day it might be the Women's Christian Temperance Union or one of several charities whose mission was to help the poor. But only the *deserving* poor. Livy had learned there was a difference. If you were a poor woman and wore your skirts high enough to show your ankles, or if you touched a drop of liquor, or if you weren't a regular churchgoer, you were *not* deserving. No matter how badly your family needed assistance.

Many of the ladies in the South End, including the mothers of Livy's friends, belonged to at least one such group, but Livy didn't know of any who were as active as her mother. The way Mum talked, the organizations would fall apart if she weren't there to run things. Dad had often told her that they would get along fine without her. His words had angered her and made her more determined to make herself indispensable.

Most of the time Livy didn't pay attention to the topics the ladies were discussing, but now and then some of them would get riled up. Arguments would break out. At such times, Mum would always have the last word.

Livy wished she could listen in on the ladies after they left the house, or on the rare occasions when her mother couldn't attend a meeting. Like the rumours that Beth's mother had brought up about Dad. How many similar conversations took place behind Mum's back?

A knock on the door, and Will came in. "Hear anything interesting?"

"Not yet. But I haven't been paying attention."

"Did Mum get things organized ahead of time?"

Livy shrugged. "I tried to help but couldn't do anything right. You know how she is. Then I got sent to my room."

"Why? Did you break another vase?"

"What?" Her eyes widened. "You knew?"

"Kathleen told me. She was *here*, Livy. She heard the crash, saw you leave the house, and was cleaning up the broken glass when Mum came home. You know the rest."

"Why didn't she tell Mum the truth?"

"She did. Mum didn't believe her. It was rotten of you not to own up."

Livy lowered her head. "I did. Just now."

"About two weeks too late!"

"I never thought...."

"That's the trouble with you, Livy. You never stop to think. Imagine how disappointed Dad would be."

"You could have told me!"

"You don't need me to tell you right from wrong."

She sniffed. "Well if I'd known…."

He shook his head in disgust and left the room.

• • •

Shortly after the ladies had left, Livy's mother came in. "No supper for you tonight," she said. "You'll stay in your room until the morning. First thing tomorrow you'll go to Richmond and apologize to Kathleen."

"But Richmond is in the North End! I can't go there!"

"You *will* go. And you'll ask her to come back. It won't surprise me if she's taken on another job, or even if she refuses, after the way she's been treated. But we can hope."

Livy expected to be punished but not like this. She thought that Mum would talk to Kathleen herself. After all, she was going to be in Richmond anyway. Why should *she* have to go all that way and apologize? "I don't know how to get to Richmond," she said. "It's too far. I'll be late for school."

"You brought this on yourself, young lady. You'll make amends. You won't be late if you take the trolley but I'll write a note for your teacher just in case."

"Will you give me the trolley fare?"

"No, you'll use your pocket money."

"That's not fair!"

"Was it fair to let Kathleen take the blame? You have a lot to learn about fairness, and about consequences."

"Where does she even live? Do you know her address?"

"Hannah will give it to you in the morning." With that, she left Livy's room and started down the stairs.

"Can I at least have breakfast?" Livy called after her.

The question was met with silence.

"It *isn't* fair," Livy muttered. Well, one thing was certain. She wouldn't waste her pocket money on the trolley. She'd walk to Richmond, the whole way, even if it meant being late for school. *Hours* late. She might even dawdle to make sure she *was* late. "So there, Mum!" she yelled, and slammed the door. Straight away she felt better. Even more so when she searched through various coat pockets and found some peppermints and humbugs. Covered in lint, but still tasty.

• • •

Something woke Livy in the night and, once awake, she couldn't get back to sleep. *Hunger pains*, she thought. Her growling stomach agreed. Earlier, Will had snuck her up a cheese sandwich and a slice of Hannah's apple pie. "Hannah will give you breakfast," he said. "Mum's leaving early for the North End."

"I knew it! She's going to be right there!" She punched her pillow with frustration. "Why do *I* have to go all that way?"

Will had given her a stern look. "Stop whining! It was terrible what you did to Kathleen. When are you going to grow up? Face it, Livy. The world doesn't revolve around you."

As he was leaving, he'd said, "And you're welcome for the snack. Don't bother saying thank you."

Reviewing the conversation in her mind made her even more awake. She went to the window and pulled back the blackout curtains to look outside.

It amazed her, the way the city could turn so completely black at night. The slightest sliver of light that escaped from a home could result in a fine. Worse still, it could alert the Germans and show them where to drop their bombs. They'd bombed towns along the coast in Britain using zeppelins. Even London had been bombed. That was two years ago, and now *airplanes* were bombing Britain. How could a city be protected from the air? It was too horrible to think about.

There'd been a storm earlier in the week, with sleet piling up only to melt away by the following day. Now the sky was clear. A half moon shone over the harbour. Livy looked to the lighthouse on McNabs Island and watched its light shine across the black waters.

Every five seconds, a beam of light. Ships could see the light and find their way into the harbour—but not since the war. People had been afraid that German submarines would sneak in under cover of darkness and attack the city. So they'd put up anti-submarine nets that stretched from one end of the harbour to the other, and gates that could be opened at certain times of the day to allow friendly ships to enter. Not at night, though. If ships arrived too late, they had to spend the whole night outside the gates.

How many are out there tonight? Livy wondered. She imagined how relieved the crews must feel when they finally reached the safety of the harbour.

Every five seconds, a beam of light. Beyond the island, beyond the light, the Atlantic Ocean.

Where journeys start and end, Dad used to say.

The words reminded her of a family picnic they'd had in Point Pleasant Park. Years ago, when she and Will were little. Dad had said that his journey from Germany to Canada had ended when his ship sailed into Halifax Harbour. He hadn't known it at the time, but his journey as a husband, father, and Canadian citizen had been about to begin.

"Because you met Mum," Livy had said, knowing the story.

"And then you got married," said Will.

Much to their surprise, their parents had kissed. Right in front of them! On the beach in a public park! She and Will had giggled and covered their eyes.

Livy swallowed the lump rising in her throat.

Another beam of light. She wished the night weren't so clear. Her mood longed for the mournful sound of foghorns.

CHAPTER 5

Thursday, December 6, 1917
8:00–8:45 A.M.

Almost feels like September, Will thought as he left the house. Except for a bit of fog, the sky was clear and there was no snow on the ground. It was a fine morning, unusually mild for December.

He walked briskly towards Citadel Hill, wondering if he should dare skip school and spend the whole day watching ships. *Better not,* he decided, remembering a French exam he had that morning. Not to mention a growing number of black marks against his name for being late. His excuse of having to get material for his weekly editorials could only go so far, especially since there'd been rumblings of students becoming bored with his stories about ships and marine traffic. Mr. Jeffreys, the teacher in charge of the school's newspaper, had even suggested that Will "expand his horizons" and tackle some new topics. Like what? The number of socks and balaclavas knitted by the Junior Red Cross? The number of Victory Bonds the school had sold? Important topics to be sure, but they were covered elsewhere in the paper. And they were hardly editorial material.

He had to admit that his piece about the Junior Cadet Corps had been well received. Being a cadet himself, he could write more about them. But only if they did something interesting. Who wanted to read about their drills or physical exercises? Or how well they could march in step or polish their boots?

He spotted Henry at the top of the hill and ran up the rest of the way. "Anything new?" he asked, taking out his binoculars.

"Just got here," Henry said. "There's a ship coming in that I haven't seen before."

The ship in question was on the Dartmouth side of the harbour, the side for inbound vessels. The boys could see the ship without binoculars, but Will wanted a closer look.

"*Mont Blanc*," he said, reading the name. "*White Mountain*. A French cargo ship. Looks like she's been around a long time. Hey, this should be interesting. Have a look." He handed his binoculars to Henry. "See the ship coming into the Narrows? With *Belgium Relief* printed on its side? That's the *Imo*. I stopped in at the pilot's office yesterday after school to see Edward, and he told me about her. She was supposed to leave yesterday afternoon but had to wait for the coal ship. By the time she got fuelled up, they'd closed the submarine gates and she had to stay the night. The captain won't be happy about that."

"Looks like he's making up for lost time, whoever he is," Henry said. "See the foam at the bow? She shouldn't be going that fast."

"And she's on the wrong side," said Will. "That could be a problem. Guess she moved over for some other ship and decided to stay there."

"She better move back if she doesn't want to hit the *Mont Blanc*," said Henry. Although the two ships were some distance apart, it was clear that they were heading straight towards each other.

Just then the *Mont Blanc* sounded her whistle. One blast to signal that she was staying her course. To make her intentions doubly clear, she moved even closer to the Dartmouth side to let the *Imo* pass. But instead of moving to the right as the boys expected, the *Imo* signalled with two whistle blasts that she was staying *her* course.

"What the heck?" Will was dumbfounded. "That doesn't make sense. If the *Imo* doesn't give way, the *Mont Blanc*'s going to run aground. She's some close."

More whistles sounded. Will and Henry frantically passed the binoculars back and forth. Each blast brought the ships closer together but neither one changed her course. "Someone's got to move or there's going to be trouble," said Henry. "Those two captains must be feeling pretty tense."

"Not to mention the pilots and crews," Will added.

At that very moment, both ships made a move. The *Mont Blanc* swung out to the left and the *Imo* reversed her engines.

"That's not going to help!" Will said in alarm. "The *Imo*'s going too fast! Her bow's swinging—"

And then it happened. A grinding shriek echoed across the harbour as the *Imo* rammed into the *Mont Blanc*, bow against bow, steel against steel.

"What a story!" Will cried. Hastily he scribbled in his notebook, *Deafening Screech of Metal as Two Ships Collide!!!* There'd be no complaints about a boring editorial this week.

Drawn by the sound of the collision, people were climbing the hill to see what was going on. The *Imo* hadn't just struck the *Mont Blanc*, she'd cut deep into her side. Now came a further grating of steel as the engines of both ships worked to pull them apart.

Will's heart pounded with anticipation. When the *Mont Blanc* was finally free, he gave a loud sigh of relief. "I wouldn't have missed that for anything! But I'm right glad it's over."

He'd spoken too soon. Dense clouds of smoke were rising into the air, shot through with flashes of red flame. He stared, amazed. The collision was one thing. Now the ship was on fire.

CHAPTER 6

Thursday, December 6, 1917
8:00–8:45 A.M.

Livy dragged herself into the kitchen, dreading the task ahead. "'Morning, Hannah," she said. "Has Mum left?"

"Twenty minutes ago. She's meeting a colleague in town and then they're off to Richmond. Will's left too. Now, you sit down and have your breakfast so I can start clearing up."

Livy did as she was told. She poured fresh cream over her porridge and sprinkled it with brown sugar. "I have to go to Richmond," she said glumly.

"You needn't make it sound like the end of the world. I lived there myself when I came from England, before I started working for your grandparents. Plenty of nice houses with trees and gardens. Good, honest, hard-working people. Like Kathleen." She faced Livy, hands on her hips, and scowled. "I have to say it's about time you did the right thing. I love you like you were my own, but I've never been so disappointed." She handed Livy an envelope. "Here's Kathleen's address. There's a note inside from your mum and you're to bring back an answer."

Livy glanced at the address. "Where's Russell Street?"

"It runs up from the harbour to the Exhibition Grounds, just past Wellington Barracks. Don't know the exact house but you've got the number. I'd say it's up the hill above Gottingen, because Kathleen's always talking about the view."

Gottingen? Wellington Barracks? These names meant nothing to Livy. Richmond could be in Newfoundland for all she knew. It was unknown territory.

Thinking of it in that light gave her an unexpected jolt of excitement. She hurried through the rest of her breakfast, listened as Hannah gave her directions, and left the house with a sense of adventure.

The morning was as clear as the night sky had promised. The air was still, almost warm, and a red sun was lighting up the harbour. Will was no doubt on the waterfront, noting anything that moved. She wondered how often he imagined Dad standing beside him, and the conversations they might be having.

No more thinking of that, Livy. You have a mission.

She was walking through the business part of town when she heard someone call her name.

Not Lewis again! She pretended she hadn't heard and walked faster. No use. The running footsteps gaining on her from behind made it clear he was going to catch up no matter what. She spun around and faced him straight on. "What are you doing here, Lewis?"

"I was about to ask you the same question," he said, grinning. "It's quite a coincidence."

"Hardly," she snapped.

"Your school isn't this way. Where are you going?"

"I'm running an errand for my mother. Not that it's any of your business. What about you? This isn't the way to your school, either. You're following me again."

"No, I'm not!" His red face told a different story.

"Well, stop it! You're a right nuisance, Lewis Fraser. If you don't—"

"I know, I know. If I don't stop following you, you'll tell your brother and he'll beat me up. I know, but listen. There's two ships in the harbour, heading straight for each other. Did you hear the whistles? I'm going down to watch, in case they crash. You want to come?"

"I already told you, I've got an errand. I haven't got time for whistles or ships. Now get lost." She crossed the street, heading away from the harbour.

"You'll be sorry," he called after her.

"I already am after seeing you! Good riddance!"

She'd have plenty of time to go to the harbour after seeing Kathleen. But honestly, two ships about to smash into each other? It wouldn't be the first near collision. Nothing to get excited about. Will would tell her the whole story, if there was a story.

With Lewis no longer a distraction, Livy became more aware of her surroundings. Citadel Hill marked the division between the north and south ends of Halifax, and she had definitely crossed into the north.

The unpaved street she found herself on was narrow and strewn with cinders, the dingy brick buildings closely crammed together. Tattered clothing hung from clotheslines, and broken bottles and rubbish littered the gutters. The street smelled as bad as it looked. And it was noisy! Yelling, crying, clattering of one kind or another, hammering, thumping, doors slamming—how could people live here?

Men hurried by on both sides of the street. A few were sailors. Most, as far as Livy could tell, looked like workers on their way to the docks or the railway or the factories, or wherever else they worked. A woman with a baby waved at her from an upstairs window. Livy lowered her gaze, embarrassed and a little uneasy. How many other people were watching her from their windows?

Is this where Mum comes to visit? she wondered. *Does she actually go inside these buildings and talk to these people? Is this where she decides if they're deserving?* Livy knew the terms the society ladies used. *Slums. Working class.* The *teeming north* filled with large families packed into small rooms. She looked around her and shuddered.

Is this where Mum gives out her pamphlets? No matter how hard she tried, Livy could not picture her mother talking about women's rights on this street. Dad hadn't liked her doing that. He'd called the Halifax Red Cross a "hotbed of suffragettes." Women getting the vote? He would have none of it.

Kathleen had been interested though. Livy had often overheard her mum talking to Kathleen about the importance of education for young women, and had given her pamphlets to pass out around Richmond. Kathleen had also taken posters to put up on notice boards, informing women about public meetings. Livy saw no such posters here.

"Step aside, Miss!"

Livy jumped back to make way for a horse-drawn wagon. In her haste, she tripped over a broken tricycle and fell hard on her knees, scraping her hands on the cinders. She winced with the pain and bit her lip to keep from crying.

Anger rose up inside. How could her mother send her to Richmond, knowing full well she'd have to walk through dangerous areas like this one? She didn't even know where she was. She'd forgotten Hannah's directions, except for Gottingen Street, Wellington Barracks, and stupid Russell Street. Was she on it already? She hadn't seen a street sign. She wanted to scream at her mother, *How could you do this to me?*

Voices argued inside her head.

It wasn't Mum's fault. Not *this* part at any rate. Mum had told her to take the trolley. Walking had been Livy's idea. She'd wanted an adventure.

Well you're having one now. So buckle down and get on with it.

She got up shakily, brushed off her hands, and was examining them for cuts when an outburst of laughter caught her attention. When she looked up she saw a group of ruffians a short ways up the street.

They were pointing at her, shouting rude comments and laughing. "Mind your step, Snooty Drawers! What are you doing here? You lost or something? Cat got your tongue?"

They were carrying school satchels but showed no intention of hurrying off to school. What's more, they were standing directly in her path. She had to stop. To cross the street or turn back the way she'd come was to admit she was afraid.

She stood tall, straightened her shoulders, and gave them what she hoped was a confident, South End sort of look. "Is this—" Her voice faltered. She cleared her throat and tried again, this time more forcefully. "Is this Russell Street?"

A redheaded boy, the oldest and toughest-looking one in the group, repeated her question, mimicking the way she spoke. He even went so far as to straighten his shoulders and raise his chin, the way she had done. The others found this hilarious.

"Russell Street, is it?" a surly boy asked when they'd had enough of the copycat game. "Who wants to know?"

They'd circled her now, and were firing questions at her.

"Yeah, Snooty Drawers. What's happening down Russell Street?"

"You got a name? You're a long ways from home, aren't you?"

"You want Russell Street, it'll cost you." The toughest one again. "How much you got?"

"Shut up, you lot!" Another redhead, this time a girl about Livy's age, strode into the group and pushed the boys aside. Her two long braids, neatly tied with ribbons, gave her the appearance of an ordinary schoolgirl, but she looked and sounded every bit as tough as the boys. For a minute, Livy wasn't sure which one she should fear the most.

"Marty!" the girl shouted at the oldest one. "Mum says you'll get a right good licking if you're not upstairs in two ticks."

Marty hustled off and the other boys stepped back to give the girls space.

"Don't mind them, South End Girl," the newcomer said. "They're full of noise and boredom."

She had the largest and bluest eyes Livy had ever seen, and the most penetrating and unsettling stare. She eyed Livy from head to toe, taking in her appearance—especially her wool coat—with such scrutiny, Livy felt even more nervous than she had before.

"Is that velvet trim on your coat?" the girl said. Without waiting for an answer, she ran her fingers over the trim on the cuffs and collar. "Lawdy-dawdy! Pearl buttons, too, I reckon. I'd give anything for a coat like that."

You're not getting mine! Livy wanted to say. She looked at the brown sweater coat the girl was wearing and wondered if she was about to suggest a trade, or if she was expecting Livy to offer her coat in return for directions.

Livy was about to make a run for it when the girl lowered her hand and said, "So. You looking for Russell Street? It's up there or down there, depending." She waved her arm in two directions. "It's not far. Runs up the side of the barracks. Why you going there?"

"I'm taking a message to someone," Livy said. She felt braver, now that the girl had stopped admiring her coat. "What about Gottingen Street? Is it far from here?"

"Gottingen? One block that way." She pointed up the hill. "Russell crosses it. I can take you if you like. Doesn't matter if I'm late for school." She took Livy's arm in a friendly way. "I'm Jane."

"Don't call her Janie or she'll hit you," the smallest boy piped up.

Jane ignored him. "What's your name?"

"Olivia, but everyone calls me Livy."

"I'll call you Liv," she said, with an impish grin. They hadn't taken two steps before they stopped, riveted by a horrendous clanging of metal.

"What's *that*?" Livy asked.

Jane was quick to react. "Something's happening down the harbour! C'mon, boys! You too, Liv!" Without another word she ran off, racing the boys down the hill.

Two sailors came running out of a building, forcing Livy to jump aside to avoid being knocked over. "Sorry, lass," one said. "Did you see what happened?"

She shook her head. Had Lewis been right? Had the ships crashed into each other?

All along the street, people were appearing in doorways and windows, wondering what had happened. "Did you hear that? What's going on? Sounds like a collision! Came from the harbour. Hurry up, get your coat, let's go see!"

Livy ran up to the nearest intersection and checked the street sign: GOTTINGEN. *Not far to go now*. Never mind what was happening at the harbour. She wanted to get back to the South End and never set foot in Richmond again. At least Kathleen didn't live on that awful street with those awful kids. Thank heavens the girl had arrived.

She was on Gottingen now, walking alongside the upper wall of Wellington Barracks. The streets running up from Gottingen were wider and tidier than the ones she'd just left. It was a nicer neighbourhood altogether. Of course it didn't have the elegant tree-lined avenues and mansions of the South End, but the wooden houses looked decent enough, with painted doors and window frames, and curtains at the windows.

And there, at last, was Russell Street. Looking down the hill to the harbour, Livy could see the two ships that had collided. One was on fire! There were people everywhere, watching from the street or on the docks, some even standing on flat rooftops for a better view.

No time to dawdle. She stepped up to a woman watching from her front yard and showed her the address written on the envelope. "Excuse me, ma'am. Do you know where I can find this house? It's where the Grants live."

"You mean Kathleen and the kids? I sure do. It's that yellow house across the street from the church. See it? You won't find Kathleen at home though. She's got a plum job working in the South End."

Not right now, she hasn't. Livy didn't say the words out loud but thanked the woman and ran across to the house. One minute in, one minute out, and she'd be on her way. This time, she'd pay the five cents and take the trolley. The sooner she left the North End, the better. Even if it meant missing the spectacle of the fire.

CHAPTER 7

Thursday, December 6, 1917
8:50 A.M.

The entire foredeck of the *Mont Blanc* was in flames. A cloud of black smoke rose into the sky.

"They'll never put that fire out!" Will exclaimed. "Looks like they're abandoning ship. Can you see?" He handed his binoculars to Henry. "They're lowering the lifeboats. Making short time of it, too. You think they know something we don't?"

"Like the ship's carrying ammunition? Can't be. There's no red flag."

"True enough, but ships haven't been flying a red flag since the war started. Why let the Germans know what they're carrying?"

"Hard to make things out through the smoke," Henry said, "but looks like they've got barrels on deck. Do you think they're full of fuel? The crew isn't wasting any time."

The sailors were in a frantic hurry—climbing down ladders, sliding down ropes, practically jumping into the lowered lifeboats.

"That looks like Captain Mackey!" Henry handed the binoculars back to Will. "See, getting into the lifeboat? What do you think?"

Will peered through the glasses and focused on the man. It was impossible to make out small details, like the pilot's bushy mustache, but the stocky build looked familiar. "I think you're right," he said. "If it is, he'll tell us about it."

Many of the crew were waving wildly to sailors watching from the decks of nearby ships. "Looks like they're yelling something," said Will.

"Like what? *The ship's on fire*?"

Will laughed. "Whatever it is, it'll be in French. It's a French ship, remember."

"Yeah, but the pilot's English."

The lifeboats were moving at an alarming speed towards the Dartmouth shore. *Why the rush*? Will wondered. *They've already escaped from the fire*.

Meanwhile, the blazing *Mont Blanc* was drifting closer and closer to the Halifax side.

"There go the sirens," Will said. "The pumper truck will be on its way. I don't envy the firemen, facing a blaze like that."

"Let's go!" Henry said excitedly. "We've got to get down there!" He picked up his satchel and was off down the hill before Will had a chance to respond.

For a moment Will stayed where he was, fixated by the sight. The fire was spectacular. Bigger, brighter, more colourful than any fireworks he'd ever seen. Not merely red, blue, and orange flames, but shades of green, yellow, and pink—colours that looked even more vibrant against the billowing black smoke.

The clock on the City Hall tower showed ten minutes before nine. He'd have to leave now if he wanted to get to school on time, but he wouldn't miss this for anything. From the looks of things, everyone felt the same way. Women and children were running down to the waterfront. Businessmen and office workers were coming out of buildings and joining him on the hill. Crews in the harbour were lining up at the deck rails to watch the burning ship.

He scribbled a few more notes, hardly able to believe his luck. *Mont Blanc a Blazing Inferno!!!* Rather than being punished for being late, he'd be congratulated for recording such an event. His article would be a winner. But Henry was right. To capture the full force of the drama, Will needed to get closer to the action.

CHAPTER 8

Thursday, December 6, 1917
8:55 A.M.

Here goes. Summoning her courage, Livy knocked on the door of the trim, two-storey house. Waited. Then knocked again, this time more loudly.

A voice inside hollered, "Tommy, Peter, one of you—get the door!"

Livy heard the clattering of footsteps coming down a flight of stairs. Eager young voices were shouting, "There's a ship on fire, Kay! You've got to come see!"

"Just answer the door!"

"We *are*!"

The door flung open, and Livy found herself looking down at two dark-haired boys. They appeared to be between five and eight years old, and their faces were flushed with excitement. After a quick glance at her face, the older one yelled, "It's some girl I don't know!" Then he turned and ran back upstairs.

"What girl? Didn't you let her in? Tommy Grant, I'm going to wring your neck!"

The younger boy, still standing in the doorway, gave Livy a shy smile. "That's my brother, Tommy. He's always getting into trouble. I'm Peter. Who are you?"

"I'm Livy."

"You can come in if you want. I'm going back upstairs to watch the fire. Do you want to see it?" His little face lit up. "It's spectac'lar! You won't believe it!" He took off down the hall before she could respond.

Livy stood for a moment, wondering what to do. She was looking down a hallway with doors opening off to either side. At the far end was a kitchen. Should she knock again or just walk in? Was it Kathleen she'd heard, or someone else?

She was about to step inside when Kathleen appeared, holding a toddler on her hip with one hand and carrying a bowl of porridge in the other.

"Well!" Kathleen was clearly taken aback. "I never expected to see you here. If you've come to apologize you're ten days too late." She turned and headed back to the kitchen.

"Wait!" Livy said, following her. "I know you must hate me and I don't blame you because it was my fault. I should have owned up right away, but I didn't until yesterday and now Mum wants you to come back. We all do. And Mum says she's going to pay you more." She winced inwardly. What made her say that? Her mother had said no such thing. "Here's a letter from Mum. She's sorry for how she treated you, but not as sorry as I am." There. It was done. She could go, as soon as Kathleen gave her an answer.

Kathleen scoffed. She set the toddler on the floor. "Stay put," she said firmly.

The little girl wailed in protest but stopped when a black-haired puppy with a white nose and four white paws scampered out of his basket and began to lick her face.

"Kay, come see the fire!" the boys were yelling. "It's right close to the pier now. Hurry up, and bring Clara!"

"And the girl!" one of the boys added.

Peter. Livy recognized his voice and smiled.

"Get down here!" Kathleen brushed a stray hair from her forehead, grabbed the letter from Livy, and set it on the table. "I don't have time for this now. You want to make it up to me, come back at a more convenient time. Better yet, take off your coat and make yourself useful." She handed Livy the bowl of porridge. "Feed this one while I fetch the boys." She left the kitchen and ran upstairs, shouting, "Last warning, you two! Get down here *now*. I won't have you late for school."

Livy was at a loss, torn between the desire to leave and the need to make amends. In the end, the latter won out. She didn't know the first thing about feeding a young child, but how hard could it be?

She took the puppy away from the toddler, who responded with another wail. "All right, have it your way." Livy gave back the puppy, picked up the girl, and sat at the table with both on her knee. "Are you Clara?" she asked.

The little girl nodded, pointed to her chest, and said, "*Tawagant.*"

Clara Grant. "And your puppy's name?"

"*Noman.*"

"Clara Grant and Norman. Nice names. I'm Livy."

"*Ibby*?"

"That's right. How old are you, Clara?"

"*Most two!*" she said proudly, holding up two fingers.

Almost two. "Do you want some porridge?"

"*No!*" Clara made a face and pushed the bowl aside.

"Well, let's have some anyway. I bet Norman would like some." Livy took a spoonful of porridge and coaxed Clara into opening her mouth before Norman licked it all from the spoon.

"'*Dain*!" Clara laughed, enjoying the who-gets-the-porridge-first game.

Livy did it again. As they continued to play, her mind churned with questions. Had Kathleen done this every morning before she arrived at the Schneiders' house to work?

Where was her mother? Who looked after Clara during the day? Their father was presumably at work, but where? Livy was ashamed to admit that she knew nothing at all about Kathleen or her family. To her, Kathleen was the servant girl who had shown up every weekday at half past eight and left at four.

The porridge was almost finished. The boys hadn't come down for their breakfast, and Kathleen no longer seemed to be hurrying them along. Instead, judging from the excited outbursts and the sounds of oohing and ahhing, she was enjoying the fiery spectacle as much as her brothers.

"Last spoonful," Livy said. "Let's give it to Norman, shall we? Then we'll go and see the fire."

"*Noman too?*" said Clara.

"Yes, he can come too."

Suddenly, the puppy scrambled out of Clara's grasp and leapt to the floor.

Clara's smile vanished and her eyes widened. "*Whaddatboom*?" she said.

Livy heard it too. And felt it. A deep, resonating roll of thunder. Not from the sky, but from under the ground. *How strange*, she thought. She looked at the windows above the sink, saw the panes of glass bending inwards, and heard an inner voice screaming, *Get down!*

She threw herself onto the floor and under the table as a storm of glass splinters flew across the room. As the ceiling and walls heaved and buckled and fell and the floor gave way beneath her.

CHAPTER 9

Thursday, December 6, 1917
9:02 A.M.

Henry's right, Will thought as he headed off towards Richmond. No use watching from a distance when he could get right close to the action. Besides, someone down at the docks might know how the fire had started. He might run into Edward, or someone else from the pilotage office, and find out if Captain Mackey had indeed been piloting the *Mont Blanc*.

As he was nearing Barrington Street he had a second thought. By the time he reached the site, the action might be over. He might get there only to see a smoking ruin. Better to avoid the crowds and stay on Citadel Hill.

He turned and ran back up. The fire was still blazing. It was unbelievable! And the heat coming from those flames? The seawater would be boiling! As for anyone getting close—well they couldn't, could they? He'd been foolish to think so. Henry wouldn't have a hope.

Does Livy know what's happening? he wondered. *Does Mum?* It was Thursday, a typical charity day for his mum, so she was sure to be somewhere in the North End. But she never went there directly. She'd meet up with a fellow volunteer downtown and they'd have a cup of tea, plan their route, and decide which residents to visit. They never started their home visits before nine o'clock, to give mothers time to get their children off to school and the breakfast dishes cleared away. But if, for some reason, she'd changed her routine and was in the North End right now, looking out from an upstairs window, she'd have a grand view. Will could compare notes with her at dinner. He could interview her and add her impressions to his article. She wouldn't care that he'd missed school, not today.

As for Livy...he felt a twinge of guilt. He should have run home the instant the fire started and urged her to come to Citadel Hill to watch. She'd never forgive him if she missed it altogether.

The *Mont Blanc* was now burning a bright red. Will shook his head in dismay. The firemen would never be able to put out that blaze. And as the ship was drifting closer to the wharves—close to Pier Six from the looks of it—and as the wharves were piled with lumber and other inflammable materials, what would happen then? What would happen when the fuel caught fire? He congratulated himself for having had the sense to return to the hill.

As that thought crossed his mind he saw a blinding flash of light. Heard the roar of thunder, the smashing of a thousand panes of glass. Felt the ground shudder. In the next instant, a fierce wind swept across the hill and knocked him off his feet.

CHAPTER 10

Thursday, December 6, 1917
after 9:05 A.M.

Something's happened.

Livy didn't know what, only that it was something terrible. Because even with her eyes closed she knew that she was buried. She knew because of the closeness, the silence, the smell of dust and ashes; the bits of glass, china, wood, and plaster that she could feel with her fingers. She knew because of the weight of wreckage piled up beside her, and beneath her, and over her face, chest, arms, legs, and feet—especially her feet, because she couldn't move them...she couldn't move.

She took a breath and coughed out plaster dust. Opened her eyes to darkness. Closed them again.

Something terrible's happened.

Her head throbbed and her eyes stung. Her nose was clogged. Her tongue felt caked with plaster. It hurt to swallow. It hurt to breathe. But she *could* breathe. Her face and upper body had somehow been shielded from the heaviest objects.

She forced her mind to go back to what she'd been doing before the something terrible. A picture rose in her mind. She was feeding a little girl, saying *open wide*, laughing at the feel of a puppy's tongue on her cheek. But that couldn't be real. Livy, with a toddler and a puppy? How could that be? It was a picture she'd seen in a storybook. It couldn't have been her.

Thunder, she remembered. Glass shattering, jingling like sleigh bells. What happened after that?

A sickness rushed into her stomach and up to her throat. She swallowed it down. Freed a hand from under the debris and gingerly brushed off her face. Dust, plaster, soot, ashes, she didn't know what else. Her hand came away sticky.

She felt cold. There was a dankness to the cold. Was she in a cellar?

She started to push the debris off her chest. Slowly, slowly, careful not to dislodge anything that might be unstable. She felt something hard and smooth. She knew, from the size and shape, that it was a piano key. A white key. She felt the cutaway part where the black key would have been, before the piano fell apart. She closed her hand around it, strangely comforted by its familiarity. It felt undamaged. She put it in her coat pocket. Why was she wearing her coat?

Clara. It suddenly came to her. She'd been in Kathleen's house, in the kitchen, feeding Clara, when the windows had bent and she'd dropped to the floor. She'd been holding Clara, holding her tight against her chest. Her heart lurched. She hadn't meant to let go but she must have, because where was Clara now?

And where's Dad? He'd be coming to rescue her. He'd take her home—

No, he wouldn't. He'd never find her here.

She opened her eyes. They felt gummy, sticky with plaster. She could see slats of light, heavy with black dust. She could make out boards, bits of broken furniture and crockery, chimney bricks, flooring, an overturned bathtub. Close by, a small bundle of clothing. She stretched an arm through broken lath and glass and when she touched the bundle, she felt the softness of a face, small hands, tangled hair.

"Clara," she whispered, "wake up." Inch by inch she eased the body towards her. It felt warm. That was a good sign, wasn't it? *Please, God, please let someone find us and dig us out, please before it's too late....*

She opened her mouth to cry for help but no sound came. Had she lost her voice? How would anyone find her if she had no voice?

Had Kathleen been buried? What about the boys, Peter and Tommy? They'd been upstairs. They could be somewhere in the rubble, unconscious but alive.

"Clara..." She stroked the curly head. No response. She nudged the shoulder. No response. *She can't be dead. She hit her head and blacked out and in a minute she'll wake up and cry and someone will hear her.*

"Wake up, Clara!" She nudged her again. *What if she doesn't? What will I tell Kathleen? Where* is *Kathleen? Why doesn't somebody come?*

She had to do something. Scream or move or bang on something. But her feet were pinned down. She was afraid to bang in case the wreckage shifted, in case whatever was shielding her face came crashing down. Her throat burned when she swallowed. She couldn't raise her voice above a whisper.

CHAPTER 11

Thursday, December 6, 1917
after 9:05 A.M.

What happened?

Will was at a loss. One minute he was watching a ship burning in the harbour. The next minute he was on the ground. He remembered seeing, hearing, feeling several things at once—a flash of light, thunder crashing, shuddering, a tornado-like wind—then nothing.

His ears were ringing and his head hurt from his fall. One leg was twisted underneath him. He straightened it, wincing with the pain, afraid it might be broken. It didn't seem to be. A cramp, like pins and needles.

He took his time standing up. Looked to the north, to the enormous black cloud looming overhead, and saw to his horror that the entire north end of the city was gone. Flattened. Demolished.

"Oh my god...." Had the Germans attacked? Dropped a bomb? Shelled the city from the harbour?

He couldn't think, couldn't move, couldn't look away from the cloud, from the black rain falling.

The clanging of fire bells and ambulance sirens broke the silence and shook him out of his stupor. He had to get home. Home and a cup of tea with Livy and Hannah.

Then it hit him. How could he have forgotten? Livy wasn't at home. She'd been sent to Richmond.

He struck off down the hill, picturing the route he had to take. *Down the hill, left onto Barrington, straight through to Russell Street, then left again....*

He knew the way because he'd secretly gone to Kathleen's house sometime in September. It was a few days after she'd arrived late at his house for work. "I bashed my knee," she'd told him. "Tripped over a cobblestone on our street. That's Russell Street I'm talking about. First street up from the railway station, just past Wellington Barracks, if you ever want to walk me home." She'd laughed, seeing him blush. But he'd been angry, not embarrassed. The way she'd flirted with him, treating him like a child.

He wanted to run, but couldn't. The streets were rivers of broken glass and he was forced to pick his way carefully.

Buildings were still standing but every window of every shop, bank, church, and warehouse had shattered.

The farther he got from the business part of town, the worse it became. Houses had collapsed or been blown off their foundations. In the distance, houses were on fire.

The snapping of live wires made him start. He tripped over what remained of a piano keyboard, its black and white keys blown apart and scattered. He thought of Livy playing the piano and a cry caught in his throat. He wasn't one for praying but if there was ever a time, it was now. *Please, God. Please let Livy be safe.*

Day had instantly turned into night. Dust and smoke made it hard to see and breathe. He was struggling over, under, and around white-hot chunks of metal, tangled wires, bricks, splintered telephone poles, overturned motorcars, lampposts, broken furniture, iron fences, fallen trees, the bodies of animals and people. Some of the bodies, some of the survivors, were naked, the blast having torn off every stitch of clothing, even shoes. Clothing that remained had been shredded into rags.

Bodies and parts of bodies. On the street, in the rubble, buried or half buried, people wounded but alive, begging for help.

Rescuers with flat wagons and empty carts were struggling to get into the area to transport the injured to hospitals. Ambulances, trucks, carts, and motorcars, already loaded with the wounded or the dead, were fighting to get out. Soldiers and volunteers were searching for survivors in the wreckage of their homes.

Later, Will promised. After he'd found Livy, after he'd taken her home, he'd come back and help.

Survivors moved in a daze, their eyes vacant. Faces and bodies were cut and bleeding, coated with the oily black rain.

Will pressed on. *Stay strong. Stay calm. You can write about it later for the newspaper.* But that was his reporter's voice and this wasn't shipping news. He did not feel calm.

The scale of the devastation was impossible to grasp. How would he ever find his sister? If she were blackened and bleeding like the others, how would he recognize her?

It was carnage. It was No Man's Land. It was the trench warfare he'd read about in newspapers. He'd seen pictures and newsreels. But no words or pictures could convey the smells, the sounds, the shivery, sickening feel of horror. This was what boys only three years older than himself were facing in France. Surviving, if they were lucky, only to face more of the same the next day and the next. But over there, they weren't stumbling over the bodies of women or children or babies.

A man grabbed his arm. "We're under attack," he said. "The Germans have dropped a bomb. Just you wait, there'll be another one."

Another man argued, "It wasn't a bomb. It was that burning ship that exploded. But you can bet it was a German who started the fire, right after he rammed into the other ship. Remember the collision? That's when it started."

The collision, Will remembered. *A lifetime ago.*

He approached a woman standing beside a cradle that had somehow remained intact. Blood flowed from a gash on her head, and one arm dangled uselessly at her side. "Look at this," she said, indicating the cradle. "Not a scratch on it. How can that be possible?" She reached out her good arm and clasped Will's hand. "Where did the baby go? Can you help me find the baby?"

"I'm sorry," Will said. "My sister...."

He stepped aside to let a wagon go by, surprised to see that it was empty and heading in the wrong direction. Why was that? Then he saw that it wasn't the only one. Vehicles that had been going into the North End to transport the injured were now turning around and going back out. Men who'd been helping with the rescue work were doing the same, leaving the helpless behind. Streams of people, including soldiers and policemen, were rushing by, yelling, "The magazine's on fire! It could go up any minute!"

Will's instincts told him to follow the others, but he couldn't give up now. He'd passed the train station, now lying in ruins, and the railway yards, where cars had been hurled from the tracks, and the tracks twisted beyond recognition. Russell Street could not be far.

"Did you see the wave?" A man grabbed him by the arm, forcing him to stop. "Never seen anything like it. Twenty foot high, picking up ships and tossing them—"

"A *tsunami*?"

The man pointed to a rowboat on top of a wrecked house. "See that? It was tied to a wharf an hour ago." Without warning, he dropped Will's arm and moved off to another man. "Did you see the wave? It was picking up bodies…."

Will moved on, noticing more evidence of the tsunami. Mooring lines, gravel, and broken shells from the harbour bottom, the reek of dead fish.

A commotion broke out as two soldiers on horseback appeared, ordering people to leave their houses and go to open ground.

"We can't!" people shouted in alarm. "Not while people are buried!"

"You can't save them now, it's too late!" the soldiers said. "The munitions are going to blow up!"

The men heeded the warning and joined the fleeing crowds.

Frantic, Will broke into a stumbling run. He fought his way through the crush of people, ignoring their warnings about another explosion. He was heading up the north side of the barracks. This was Kathleen's street, or what used to be her street. He remembered that her house was yellow, on the other side of Gottingen, close to a church.

The smell of smoke was getting stronger. He could hear the crackle of flames and feel the heat. It was clear to him now that fear of another explosion wasn't the only reason for panic. The fires were spreading. Not only from the harbour area, but from within the collapsed wooden houses where stoves had toppled over and chimneys had fallen down. Sparks had caught onto dry tinder. Shards of burning metal had landed onto rooftops and set them ablaze.

He'd reached the top corner of the barracks. He saw the ruins of a church and knew at once that Kathleen's house was close by. It came to him that the church had to be St. Joseph's, on Gottingen Street, and Kathleen's house was two houses up from the corner—and now, engulfed with flames.

"Livy!" he screamed, rushing over. Knowing it was useless. Knowing that if she were inside, she would be past saving.

Smoke stung his eyes and burned his lungs. He couldn't go any farther. The heat drove him back.

He cried out in despair. What had he been thinking? To go tearing off like a mad fool—he should have used his head. Livy had hated the very thought of going to Richmond. She would have hurried to Kathleen's, done what she had to do, and left straight away. At this very moment she was probably in her classroom. How would she feel if her brother were killed now because he'd ignored the warnings to leave?

He joined the desperate survivors, praying that he would get out of the area before it was too late.

CHAPTER 12

Thursday, December 6, 1917
after 9:05 A.M.

Whimpers.

Livy opened her eyes and listened. High-pitched whimpers. A faint scratching and scrabbling that knocked over a board and filled her nose and mouth with yet more dust. She spat it out and coughed loudly.

At the sound of Livy's coughing, Clara stirred and opened her eyes. They stared at Livy, huge with fear.

Livy's heart leapt with relief. "It's all right, Clara. Don't be afraid." Every word was an effort, but she forced them out, trying to build up the strength to alert whoever was making the sounds.

They sounded close. Then farther away. To her left, to her right, sometimes up above.

"Help!" The word came out a cackle.

The sounds were louder. No longer whimpers, but excited yaps. *It must be Clara's dog, Norman. He knows we're here, he's trying to reach us….* Frantic scratching. A running back and forth. And now—*oh please, please*—she heard the movement of debris and men's voices.

"Bring a torch—there's someone down here! The dog's trying to get in!"

Livy coughed to clear her throat and tried again to shout "Help!"

"Careful!" someone yelled. "Don't knock anything over! Get a rope around that bathtub!"

She smelled smoke. Something, somewhere, was burning. "Help! HELP!"

Beside her, Clara let out a shrieking cry.

"Hurry, hurry!" More shouting from above, and a man calling down, "Hold on, sweetheart. We're coming."

The rescuers laboured until enough rubble had been cleared away for Livy to look up and see a black sky. *Nighttime.* A torch lit up a man's face. "Dad," she murmured. "I knew you'd come…."

The rescuers were getting closer. "Careful! Steady! Don't let that bathtub shift—move that beam off her feet—careful! Easy does it—"

Norman had scrambled through the rubble and was licking their faces. *Thank god,* Livy thought. *Dad's here and we're safe.* Strong arms reached down and gently lifted them up.

Livy looked around her and gaped. The air was thick with black smoke. Flames were shooting from buildings—what was left of buildings—a short distance away. There were boulders lower down on the street—what used to be a street—and there were signs of water, as if the harbour itself had been hurled onto the land. She was in a different world. Her rescuers were soldiers. Her father was not among them.

"You're safe, lass," one of the soldiers was saying. "You're covered with cuts and scratches but you're safe. Can you walk?"

She stared at him, stunned. *Walk?* She took a few shaky steps.

"No broken bones, then," he said. "That's a wonder. And thanks to that dog of yours, we got you out of the wreckage just in time. The burning coals from the stove were already catching on. Now you and your sister have got to get out of here."

Sister? Livy had been trying to follow what the soldier was saying but his words were nothing more than sounds, until now. "She's not my sister…" she started to explain, but he wasn't listening.

"Go to the Commons, somewhere open," he said. "Follow the others, you'll be fine." He put Clara in her arms and moved on.

Fine?

She watched the soldiers approach a group of people standing beside another collapsed house. This time they didn't ask if anyone might be buried, or listen for sounds, or move wreckage to search. They moved urgently from one group to another, ordering everyone to leave the area. Soldiers on horseback were doing the same. Why had they stopped searching? Livy wanted to shout at them, to tell them that Kathleen and her brothers could be in the rubble where she'd been buried. They probably *were* in the rubble—she was certain she'd heard them—and if the soldiers didn't come back, she'd have to do the searching herself. Because what would happen to Clara if she couldn't find Kathleen?

She had to stay. She owed it to Kathleen to stay and search before the fire really got going. But her feet were moving of their own accord, into the tide of people heading for the Commons.

Was that her father up ahead? If only she could reach him....

Clara began to cry.

Livy tried to say something soothing, but the words came out harsh and gravelly. She gave Clara a comforting pat.

"*Wan Noman*," Clara cried.

Livy turned and spotted the puppy a few steps behind, limping along on his chubby legs, his paws bleeding from the broken glass. As she went to pick him up, she looked back the way they had come and saw the wreckage of Kathleen's house. Like the others on the street, it was in flames.

She gave the puppy to Clara to hold, and stumbled on with both in her arms. She wanted to tell Clara that she was taking them home to her house. But she couldn't find her voice. Her throat felt as though it were full of ashes and burning coals.

She moved in a trance. One slow, shaky step at a time.

Nothing was recognizable. There were no buildings, no streets, no telephone poles or lampposts, only the remains. Broken, burning, twisted, mangled. Nothing, no one, was whole. She moved through a scene of horror, occupied by the injured, the dead, and the dying. It was beyond understanding.

Anyone who could move was leaving the area, desperate to escape the fires and the fear of another attack. People were using anything they could find to transport small children and wounded people unable to move. Carrying them on doors or boards, pushing them in wheelbarrows or baby carriages, pulling them on toboggans or wagons.

That's what Livy needed. Clara had fallen asleep and was growing heavier by the minute. She loosened the child's grip on Norman, fearful that he might suffocate in Clara's arms.

She picked up fragments of conversation as she moved with the crowd, most of it incomprehensible. Her mind wasn't working properly. But one word stood out from the rest—*Germans. How did this happen? The Germans.*

Who caused it? The Germans. A burning ship. A bomb on the ship. Put there by a German. It always came back to the Germans.

She ignored the voices and concentrated on the knowledge that each step was taking her closer to home. Hannah would be there, and Mum, and Will, and for a moment she could pretend that the horror had never happened.

CHAPTER 13

Thursday, December 6, 1917
after 9:05 A.M.

Will was stunned. With a second explosion expected to happen, and survivors still buried, and ambulances unable to reach the injured because of the crowds—it was too much to comprehend. Once he got home, he would think. At least his mother would be safe. If she wasn't at home, then she'd already be organizing food and shelter for the homeless.

She and her multiple organizations would have their work cut out for them, and they wouldn't be wasting time deciding who was worthy or deserving. If there was ever a time for the South End to forget about class divisions, it was now.

People would need housing, for one thing. Once he got home and ensured that everyone was safe, he'd find Kathleen and the rest of her family and they'd all be welcome in his house. There was room enough for a dozen people. It was the right thing to do. His father would have done the same.

He felt a stinging behind his eyelids. *Smoke*, he told himself. *Not tears*. He couldn't cry. Except for small children, not a single person he'd seen had been crying. The shock was too great.

Did Kathleen survive? What about Henry? He was going to the harbour to get closer to the fire.... If he made it that far, could he possibly have survived?

Will's mind was spinning. What if he'd been wrong about Livy? What if she hadn't been in a hurry to leave? What if she'd been delayed? Of course! *Stupid!* He kicked himself for not thinking of it sooner. She would have heard the collision and run down to see what was happening like everybody else. She would have seen the fire and stayed to watch.

Just then someone bumped into him. He turned sideways to catch his balance—and there she was.

No. It couldn't be. He'd been thinking about her and now he was imagining her. He was in shock. Hallucinating.

He rubbed his eyes, shaken by the sight. The girl wasn't Livy. She was holding a child and a puppy. Bent over by their weight, she looked as though she might drop to her knees at any moment. She looked like so many others.

Her eyes blank, her hands cut and bleeding, her face blackened, her fair hair streaked with blood and plaster and oily soot. She appeared to be in a trance. Like so many others, she looked lost.

He was starting to move away when he heard a strangled cry. "Will...wait."

"*Livy?*" He spun around and caught her before she fell.

CHAPTER 14

Thursday, December 6, 1917
Late morning

The house was on fire.

Livy smelled smoke, heard the snap and pop of flames, and felt a suffocating heat.

It was hard to breathe. Something was pinning her down. She opened her mouth to scream but couldn't make a sound. Opened her eyes. All was in darkness.

I'm still buried.

Her heart raced with panic. Until she realized that there was nothing hard or jagged around her, only softness, a heavy softness piled over her head and around her body. Her quilt. She was in bed, tangled up in her flannel nightdress and smothering in the eiderdown. No wonder she felt as if she were burning. She flung it off her face and saw the glow of a fire, safely contained in a fireplace across the room.

I'm home. For the moment, that was all she needed to know. She lay still, waiting for her heartbeat to slow down.

The room was dark, the blackout curtains drawn. *It's night*, she thought. *How long have I been asleep? And who's doing all the hammering?* People didn't work at night, not on her street. She pulled the chain on her bedside lamp, puzzled when the light didn't come on.

After a few more minutes of lying still, she untangled herself, threw off the quilt, and sat up. Wiggled her toes and flexed her feet. Bruised, but not broken.

She got out of bed, putting her full weight on both legs, and winced. The muscles were sore.

A gust of cold wind blew in, causing the fire in the grate to flare up. She shivered. Had she left the window open? That was careless. She went over and parted the curtains a crack. Daylight! She must have been asleep for a day and a night and now it was the next morning.

There was no glass in the window. No glass in any of the houses across the street. Wooden sashes had been blown off and doors torn from their hinges. That explained the hammering. She saw some of the neighbours putting up storm windows or nailing boards over the empty frames. Will would have to do the same.

Now that she could see, she examined her hands. The cuts were painful, but no longer bleeding. Someone had wrapped bandages around her wrists and across her left palm. Some of her fingers were bandaged.

Looking in the mirror, she was surprised to see a bandage on her forehead. She couldn't remember how she'd cut her head.

Well, she'd better get moving or she'd be late for school. She looked around for her uniform but couldn't find it. *Mum must have put it somewhere when she put me in my nightdress.* The thought gave her pause. Since when had her mother put her to bed? Since never. Until she'd started school, it had always been Hannah.

She put on a woollen dress and a sweater and went downstairs, one step at a time. She'd scarcely left the bottom step before Hannah was rushing out of the kitchen.

"Livy!" she cried. "Thank the good Lord you're safe and sound!" She wrapped Livy in her arms, hugging her so fiercely that Livy had to gasp for air. "Are you all right? You poor dear girl! I've been breathless with worry and—" She broke off in sobs.

"I'm fine," Livy said. Her voice trembled. Her throat burned. Every word was a struggle.

Hannah released her and dabbed her eyes with her apron. "Into the kitchen now, love. I made Scotch broth this morning and was just tidying up when I heard a loud bang and ten seconds later, the windows shattered. I tell you, it was a good thing the lid was on the soup, otherwise it'd be full of bits of soot and even glass."

"I'm not hungry," said Livy.

"Isn't it lucky we've got a wood-burning stove? Because otherwise, with the gas lines broken and all the power out—and look who's here! I found some of your clothes from when you were little. There's a trunk in the attic and it's chockablock. You'll want to have a look, but in the meantime that woollen sailor suit fits the bill. It's warm and cozy, compared to what she was wearing when she got here."

Livy stopped in the doorway, momentarily confused by the sight of a small child dressed in an outfit that she'd worn at that age. Then she remembered. It was Clara, Kathleen's sister. And she was playing with her puppy, Norman, in Livy's kitchen, just as she'd been doing in her own kitchen. Before the terrible thing happened.

Livy cleared her throat and tried to speak. At the sound, Norman came over to greet her. He moved slowly, as his wounded paws had been wrapped in gauze. Clara stayed put, staring at her with a puzzled look.

"Remember me?" Livy said. Her voice sounded croaky. She patted Norman and went to kneel beside the little girl. "I'm Livy."

"*Ibby*." Clara looked at the scrapes and bandages on Livy's hands and compared them to those covering her own hands and arms. "Ow," she said, touching the bandages on Livy's cheeks and chin. She then turned away from Livy and held up her arms to Hannah.

"She's confused, poor mite," Hannah said. "She'll need some time." She picked up the child and kissed her wounded cheek. "Is that better, love? You're such a brave girl." After setting her back down she said to Livy, "She's been as good as gold. I gave her a bath, scrubbed away all the black, bandaged her up, and wrapped her in a quilt. Laid her down on the sofa in the back parlour so she'd be close to me. Thought she'd be dead to the world, but she'd have none of it. Wouldn't let me out of her sight. Or the little mutt, for that matter. Is he really called Norman? His paws were so badly cut it's a wonder he can move at all. How about some soup, Livy?"

"I'm not hungry," Livy repeated. "What day is it?"

"Why, it's Thursday, love. Not yet noon."

"Thursday? But that's when I went to Richmond. It can't be the same day."

"Oh, it's the same day, all right. The worst and longest morning of my whole entire life and it's not half over. The day, I mean. And if I don't find out soon about your mum...."

"Mum? She was here, wasn't she? She treated my cuts and put me to bed."

"No, love, that was me. Don't you remember? Oh, my. I cleaned you up as best I could—had to be gentle, you know, what with all the scrapes and cuts—'cause goodness gracious, you were some black, even your hair. I washed it too, and that was a trial. It's a trial at the best of times, but I'm telling you! Caked plaster, black goop, glass splinters, and I don't know what else, all mixed in and tangled up in your hair. Blood, too, from the gash on your forehead. I'd have taken you to hospital if you'd needed stitches, but the wound isn't that deep."

Livy's head was beginning to ache. When Hannah paused for a breath, she seized the moment. "I need to know—"

"And then I dressed your wounds," Hannah continued, as if Livy hadn't spoken. "I put you to bed and lit the fire in your room to keep out the cold, you know, from the windows being blown out. You were dead on your feet, as limp as a rag doll."

"Where's Mum?" Livy tried again. It wasn't unusual for Hannah to talk non-stop, but at such a time? Livy had stopped listening. She couldn't concentrate, and it seemed that there was something Hannah was trying very hard not to say.

Hannah ignored her question. "And all that time, would you believe that Clara was right there? She stuck to me like a limpet on a rock. She was some concerned about you. Patted your hand when I put you to bed. Such a sweetheart. Look at her now—"

"Hannah, stop! Tell me where Mum is."

"I don't know!" Hannah wailed. "I wish I knew, but I don't, and I've been worried sick because she went to Richmond and I haven't heard—"

"Where's Will?" Livy's heart raced with anxiety. "I need to talk to Will. I need to find Mum!"

"He ran off to find your mum, right after he brought you home. He's also looking for Kathleen. Try to eat some more, Livy. Are you sure you're all right? You ought to go back to bed after the time you've had."

Livy rose from her seat. "I've got to help Will. Check the hospitals and the Commons—people were going to the Commons because of the other explosion—"

"Calm yourself. I know you're worried, we're all worried, but you're in no condition to go tearing off looking for your mum. We'll leave it to Will for now. I've been across to the neighbours but they don't know anything apart from the windows being shattered and the phone lines down and the electricity and gas cut off. That's all I knew until Will came home and told me what he'd seen and how he found you. I thought I'd die on the spot when he came in carrying you and Clara—"

"He carried us? *Both* of us?"

"You were in no shape to walk when he found you—that's what he told me—so he picked up the pair of you. Said he didn't know where he got the strength. But after a while he spotted a child's wagon and pulled you the rest of the way. He left the wagon outside when he got home and, as I was saying, when he came in with you and Clara in his arms, and that puppy at his heels...." She looked at Livy and burst into tears.

Clara toddled over and buried her face in Hannah's lap, a gesture that made Hannah cry even harder.

After a while Hannah took a handkerchief from her apron pocket, blew her nose, and wiped her eyes. She picked up Clara, took a moment to compose herself, and said, matter-of-factly, "There's one thing we can do, and that's cover the windows to keep out the cold. Blankets and quilts will do for now, until Will puts up the storm windows. If you can manage, you can help me with that."

"*Me hep too*," said Clara.

"Yes, love. You can help, too. There's the odd bit of broken glass that still needs sweeping. I did as much as I could. Isn't it something, how the glass mostly blew out and not in?"

Livy shook her head. "I saw the windows bending in. And then...." She stopped, unable to go on.

"Livy, you've been through a hell I can't imagine. You needn't say another word. You needn't lift a finger if you're not up to it. But honestly, love, the best thing to do is keep busy. Either that, or have a good cry."

CHAPTER 15

Thursday, December 6, 1917
Late morning

His mother wasn't at home. Considering what he'd been through, Will should not have been surprised, but he was. The thought that his strong, unshakeable mother might not have survived was a thought he wouldn't allow. If she wasn't at home, she had to be somewhere else. Possibly injured—he would allow for that. Not seriously, but enough to land her in hospital.

He'd start with Camp Hill. It was a military hospital, newly built for convalescent soldiers returning from the war, and he'd heard rescuers saying that many of the injured were being taken there.

Because of its position behind Citadel Hill, the hospital had been sheltered from the worst of the blast. Even so, like the buildings in the South End it had lost all of its windows and doors. Will was astounded to see that the openings had already been covered with boards, blankets, or tarpaper. How long had that taken? It was only an hour or so since the explosion, wasn't it? He looked at his watch and saw 9:05. That wasn't right. He must have banged it on something when he fell.

The area outside the hospital was chaos. Will gaped at the steady parade of vehicles coming and going—ambulances, motorcars, trucks, wagons, even wheelbarrows, their volunteer drivers anxious to unload the wounded so they could drive back for more. Other volunteers, armed with stretchers or anything that might serve as a stretcher, carried the wounded inside. Added to this mayhem was a frantic crowd of survivors desperate to get inside to search for family members.

Will gritted his teeth as he joined them, pushing, jostling, and elbowing his way through the open door. Once inside, he froze. His stomach reeled. How would he ever find her?

Hundreds of injured people jammed the dark corridor. Still more were crammed into offices and storage rooms. Children, babies, women, and men with all manner of terrible injuries were sitting or lying against the wall or on the floor, covering not only the width of the corridor but the entire length. Some were lucky enough to be on mattresses.

The rest were on the bare floor. There was no clear space for searchers to move except over and around or in between the injured.

Stretcher-bearers continued to bring in the wounded, setting them down wherever they could find space. Some of the stretcher-bearers, Will noticed, were recovering soldiers, barely able to walk themselves. From the looks of things, no one seemed to be in charge. There were too many wounded and not enough nurses or doctors to treat them. Volunteers were assisting wherever they were needed—and that was everywhere.

With the windows covered up, and oil lamps providing the only light, it was impossible to see clearly. How would he recognize anyone? Many faces had been horribly disfigured. Others were blackened or covered in bandages.

Not only was the hospital dark, it was freezing. Some of the wounded had had their clothing blown off by the blast and were shivering in the shredded remains. They would die of exposure if they weren't treated soon.

Will's heart dropped. "It's hopeless," he said. "I'll never find her."

"Not if you just stand there!" a nurse said sharply as she walked past. "Start looking!"

Her words snapped him out of his stupor. Steeling himself for what might lie ahead, he carried on.

It was impossible to move without disturbing someone. He lost count of the number of times he had to apologize for tripping over somebody's feet or stepping on a mattress—or once, shamefully, on someone's hand.

Yet no one reacted. In spite of their suffering and the packed conditions, there was a startling calmness amongst the wounded. No hysterical screaming or shouting, no shrieks of pain. Except for the occasional moan or whimper, all was quiet.

They must still be in shock. He wondered how long Livy would be in that state. When he'd left her with Hannah she'd been unresponsive. Hadn't said a word, hadn't seemed aware of what was going on. She'd shown a flicker of recognition when she saw Hannah, but the rest...he shook his head.

As Will stumbled through the maze of injured people, he forced himself to look at their faces. The brown-haired, middle-aged woman lying against the wall—could that be his mum? The girl who sat hugging her knees, her face partially hidden by a veil of dark hair—was that Kathleen? The boy with the missing leg—could that possibly be Henry? No, no, and no.

Keep going, he urged himself. *Keep telling yourself that Livy's alive and she needs you. Mum will need you, once you find her. Be strong and keep looking.*

The wards opening off to either side were as packed as the corridors with searchers and patients. He saw two patients to some beds, even more if they were children. Four rows of mattresses lay between the beds. In one room, he saw patients lying on mattresses under the beds.

Heaven help us if Mum ends up on a mattress on the floor. Will shuddered, and immediately felt ashamed. If his mum were to care about such a trivial matter, it would mean that she wasn't seriously injured. And that would be a good thing.

He shivered in the cold. A gust of wind parted a blanket that had been nailed over a doorway and, when he glanced inside, he saw a doctor operating on a patient. He frowned. That couldn't be right. The room was a kitchen. The patient was on a kitchen table. A nurse and a volunteer stood on either side, holding oil lamps for light. He hurried past, shaken by the sight.

"Excuse me." He stopped a young woman with a tray of surgical instruments. "Is there a list of names somewhere, of the people who've come in?"

"Are you insane?" she said. "Look around you. Everyone's too busy to be writing names."

He apologized and continued on his way. When he'd covered the first floor, he went up to the second. In every ward he heard people calling out the names of missing relatives. He did the same, though he had to wonder how the injured—especially those whose eyes were bandaged—would be able to recognize one voice amongst so many others. Added to that confusion were the sounds of nurses and volunteers giving directions, calling for supplies, pushing trolleys, and carrying trays, weaving in and out amongst the beds and people as they tried to attend to their patients.

In every ward he saw the same ghastly sights he'd seen in the hospital corridors and on the streets—broken limbs, burns, gashes on heads and faces, eyes stabbed with splinters of glass—but still no sign of his mum.

He left the last ward telling himself not to be discouraged. She could be in another hospital or on the Commons. Or she could be at Camp Hill and he'd simply missed her. He'd have to come back and try again later.

As he was leaving the hospital he heard an ambulance driver telling people that the Richmond area was safe. "That warning about a second explosion?" he was saying. "Nothing more than a rumour. A soldier told me, not ten minutes ago. So anybody looking to help, you're sorely needed in the North End."

I'll look there too, Will decided, praying that his mother would not be amongst those buried in the wreckage.

CHAPTER 16

Thursday, December 6, 1917
Afternoon

The hammering on the street had not let up. The afternoon had gotten colder and people were hurrying to cover up their windows before nightfall.

Livy had helped Hannah drape blankets over the smashed-out windows, a slow process since Clara had insisted on joining in and Norman had done his best to be underfoot. Livy herself had slowed things down at first, but once she'd had a chance to limber up, she could move and bend more easily.

After that, she'd lit a coal oil lamp and taken it up to the attic. It didn't provide much light, but a little was better than nothing. She'd rummaged through the trunk and pulled out anything that might fit Clara, surprised to discover that Mum had kept a great number of Livy's clothes from when she was little. She set aside everything that was Clara-sized and put the rest in a box to take to the Commons or to City Hall or wherever one was supposed to take such things. Before leaving the attic she'd spotted her high chair and well-loved rocking horse. Perfect for Clara.

She'd gone through the unused bedrooms on the third floor and found chests of linen, quilts, and blankets as well as boxes of toys, books, and dolls. There were other chests filled with clothing but those could wait till later.

She and Hannah were resting over a cup of tea, watching Clara ride the rocking horse, when Will came home.

"Livy!" he said. He held out his arms and embraced her. "Thank god! I didn't expect to see you up and about so soon. Are you sure you're all right?"

"I am, thanks to you. Hannah said you carried Clara and me both. How did you manage?"

"Superhuman strength," he said with a wink. "Just don't ever ask me to do it again."

Clara was tugging at his pant leg, wanting attention. He lifted her up and swung her high in the air, again and again, much to her delight.

After setting Clara back on the horse and giving Norman a scratch behind the ears, Will sat down and poured himself some tea. "I'm relieved that you're all right, the pair of you, but I'm darned if I know why. It's a wonder you're not in hospital, or worse. Someone must've been watching over you."

"It was Dad," Livy said.

Will smiled and nodded. Looked away for a moment, and turned back with a sombre expression.

"What's wrong?" Livy said. "Is it Mum? Did you find her?"

"Not at Camp Hill," he said. "But I might have missed her. It was some chaotic in that place. I didn't see Kathleen, either."

"It's early yet," Hannah added. She'd gotten up from the table and was busily making sandwiches at the kitchen counter. "They could be in another hospital. I'll do some looking myself this afternoon."

"So will I," said Livy.

"No, you're better off staying here and minding Clara." Will's voice was firm. "I don't want to worry about you, not after this morning. I've got some good news, such as it is—Richmond is safe. I'm going there later on, but now," he said, rising from his chair, "I'm putting up the storm windows. Superhuman strength, remember?"

"Oh, no you don't!" Hannah set a plate of sandwiches in front of him and forced him to sit back down. "You're not lifting a finger until you've had a sandwich. When's the last time you've eaten? Breakfast, and that was hours ago.

What good are you if you're weak with hunger? Superhuman strength, my eye. After all you've been through…." She rumpled his hair with affection, and stood watch while he finished his meal.

After that, Will went outside and put up the storm windows. He then went to the shed for a crowbar and pickaxe and, before they knew it, he was on his way to the North End.

"He's right, you know," Hannah said soon after. "It's best to keep busy. Don't worry," she added, seeing the concern on Livy's face. "The danger has passed. Didn't he say so himself? There won't be another explosion."

"You weren't there. I want to tell you, but…." She took a raspy breath and found that her chest was hurting. "I should look for Mum. She could be in Victoria General and it's not far."

"You will do no such thing," Hannah said. "It's too soon. The hospitals will be full of what you saw in the streets. *I'm* doing the searching this afternoon and that's final."

"There were no streets." She watched Clara rocking contentedly on the rocking horse. "There's more toys I can give away," she said. "And lots of warm clothes. Mum won't mind. Will she, Hannah?"

"Bless you, Livy," she said. "Of course she won't mind. She'll be proud. And if your dear dad were here—" She dabbed her eyes with her apron and sniffed. "No time for tears now. I'll clear the plates and set off for Victoria General and the Commons. The way Clara's head's drooping, she's ready for a nap. You should do the same."

Livy wanted to keep busy, not take a nap. With Clara sleeping soundly in an upstairs bedroom, she set herself the task of packing up some winter clothes. They'd be needed the most because people with no homes to go to might have to spend the night on the Commons. *The night.* Was it still, unbelievably, the same day? Every clock in the house had stopped at 9:05. It was as if time itself had stopped.

She finished going through one trunk and started on another. A fur coat lay on top, carefully wrapped in a bedsheet. She took it out, wondered briefly if her mother would ever wear it again (she already had two newer ones), and decided she wouldn't. Off it went into the third box of giveaways. A white muff made of rabbit fur went in next, only to be removed an instant later for Clara. Scarves, capes, mittens, socks, gloves, earmuffs, coats, jackets—how much did one family need? They were mostly items that she and Will had outgrown or grown tired of, but many had been worn by her parents.

She'd started on yet another trunk when she was overcome by a great weariness. After checking in on Clara, she went into her bedroom, stretched out on the bed, and nestled into her eiderdown. "I'm fine," she whispered. *Aren't I?*

Coals burned in the grate. A steady glow, until a draft stirred up a flicker of flame.

The smell took her back. The house burning around her—no, that had come later. Before that, she'd smelled smoke and smouldering coals. Felt the taste in her mouth and at the back of her throat. Moments before the soldiers had rescued her and Clara.

They hadn't been buried alone. It wouldn't go away, the thought that Kathleen and her brothers had been trapped inside and left behind.

And what about Mum? Livy hadn't said goodbye. Hadn't seen her since yesterday afternoon. Her last words had been an angry "So there," shouted out before she'd slammed the door. She'd gone to Kathleen's hating her mother for sending her there. What if she, too, was buried somewhere in the ruins?

I'm fine, she'd told Will and Hannah, but it wasn't true. How could she be fine, not knowing where Mum was or if she was even alive?

She urged herself to get up and get busy. Thinking and worrying didn't solve anything. But the room was warm and she was safe....

• • •

Will pulled another board off the pile, another length of twisted pipe, another smashed wardrobe. It was a painstaking process, clearing away debris to reveal the places where someone might be trapped. He and the other volunteers listened for the smallest sound—a gasp, a cry, a cough. When they found someone, living or dead, they lifted or pulled them from the wreckage gently, almost reverently. He couldn't escape the fact that his mother might be amongst the buried, and he wanted to think that she would be treated with the same degree of care.

The North End was feverish with activity. Rescuers struggled to make up for lost time, to recover bodies and find survivors before it was too late. All available troops, soldiers and sailors alike, had been sent to the devastated area, and there was no shortage of volunteers to assist. Armed with sledgehammers, axes, crowbars, and levers of all kinds, they tugged at wreckage and pulled out scraps of wood and metal and furniture until they were certain no bodies remained.

As he was working, Will heard more about the rumour that had emptied the area.

"The military never gave the order to evacuate," a young man said. "Know what started it? Some civilian saw smoke coming from the magazine and panicked. Spread the word about another explosion. Then other civilians took up the cry and the soldiers believed it. They probably thought they'd missed the official order. So they spread the word some more, and then the police did the same, and soon they were knocking on doors and telling people to get out."

Another man added, "Some of those poor folks—old folks a lot of them—they were sick in bed at the time of the explosion. So now they're sick and injured, and they've got to get up and leave their house. I saw this one fellow—he couldn't get up, he couldn't walk, so a couple of men picked him up and carried him, bed and all."

"I happen to know what actually happened." A third man had joined in. "A soldier told me himself. The explosion knocked over a hot water heater and a bunch of burning coals ended up on the floor. So they got a fire extinguisher to put it out. And that caused a lot of steam. Since there's smoke everywhere anyway, and steam looks enough like smoke—well, it's not hard to understand why someone would think it was a fire and panic, seeing as how it was coming from where the ammunition is stored. They didn't know that soldiers were already carrying the munitions to a safe place. The whole sorry business? Nothing more than a rumour."

"It was a lot more than a rumour," Will said. He wrestled angrily with a heavy chunk of metal. "It was a second disaster."

He thought of the people who had been trapped in collapsed or burning houses, crying for help, not knowing that a rumour had driven everyone away. He wished that he had been brave enough to stay.

Will worked steadily into the evening, wondering if the day would ever end. The darkness of the city, with its blackout conditions, made it difficult to see at the best of times. Now, with an overcast sky and wreckage everywhere, it was impossible. The searchers shone torches into piles of debris and down into basements and cellars, hoping to see signs of life, but without proper light their efforts were next to useless. Even walking in the area was hazardous.

When the frustration became too much, Will left the area and headed for the Commons. His mum could be there, possibly injured, too confused perhaps to think of going home. Kathleen could be there as well. If she'd survived, she'd be frantic about Clara. He'd like to be the one to tell her that Clara was safe.

He planned to stop at Camp Hill on the way home and have another look for his mum, in case he didn't find her at the Commons. After that, he'd stop by Henry's house. He didn't expect Henry to be there. How could he be, since he'd been heading towards the burning ship? But Henry's parents might know something. And Will could at least tell them when he'd last seen their son.

He shivered, realizing for the first time that he was cold. He'd been plenty warm while working, but now that he'd stopped, it was obvious that the temperature had fallen dramatically. People without shelter were in for a bitter night.

There were throngs of people crowding the Commons when Will got there. Some clustered around small campfires for warmth. A few were singing hymns for comfort. Others wandered from group to group, calling out names in the hopes of finding a missing loved one. Many, still in shock, huddled in the grey blankets that soldiers had provided. The same soldiers were erecting tents for those who had lost their homes.

As he was searching the crowds for a familiar face, an unexpected image came to mind—that of Kathleen's father, Mr. Grant. Will had seen him once, the time he'd walked up Russell Street to find out where Kathleen lived. He'd been standing outside her house when a tall, well-built man with a toddler on his shoulders had come galloping into the front yard, neighing and prancing around in circles. The little girl, who must have been Clara, had been shrieking with laughter and her dad had joined in with a rollicking laugh and a wide grin that revealed two gold teeth. Will had watched them, smiling, until Mr. Grant had noticed him and asked if he was looking for someone. Will had muttered something or other and walked away, embarrassed.

Was Mr. Grant amongst the crowd? Will figured he might recognize him in the daylight, barring serious injuries, but now? It would be difficult to find anyone here in the dark. Come to think of it, the hospital would be darker than it had been in the morning. Better to wait till tomorrow. For now, he'd head directly to Henry's.

His route took him past the house where Captain Mackey lived. As Will was approaching, he happened to see the captain on a ladder, putting up his storm windows. Will was certain that it was Captain Mackey he'd seen rowing away from the *Mont Blanc*. Had he been mistaken? Or had the pilot escaped from the explosion untouched? If so, it was incredible. And to have energy to spare, this late in the day and after such an experience? That really was something.

"Captain Mackey!" he said, walking over. "I'm glad to see you're all right."

The pilot acknowledged the greeting and climbed down, giving Will a friendly pat on the back. "Likewise, Will. I got some of that black stuff all over me, but nothing worse."

"Was it you I saw on the *Mont Blanc* this morning? Getting into the lifeboat?"

"It was me, all right," the captain replied. "We got to the Dartmouth side and we were in the woods when the blast came. We were knocked down and a tree fell over top of me—branches bigger than my arm—and somehow those branches landed on either side of me. Would you believe it? After that, I was walking down to the ferry and wanted to get a cap since mine was blown off, but the shops were all smashed in. And then, of all things, I ran into a man I knew, a druggist, and he gave me his cap. I came across on the ferry, stopped in at the pilot office, and went home. My oldest girl got cut up pretty bad at school. Glass in her face and her chest. Thankfully, the rest of the family is fine. What about you and yours, Will?"

"Well enough," Will said. No need to go into details. He said good night and continued down the street, wishing he'd asked the pilot what he and the crew had known that made them abandon the *Mont Blanc* with such haste. Had the crew survived? How had Captain Mackey felt when he'd looked across the harbour and seen Richmond ablaze?

The pilot had spoken in his usual chatty manner, as if it were an ordinary day. And to remember such small things as the cap and the druggist—he didn't appear to be in any kind of shock.

Then again, suffering through an ordeal like that was bound to affect people in different ways. The pilot's back-to-it attitude reminded Will of his mum after Dad had gone. She'd thrown herself into her societies and her committee work as if nothing had happened. Whatever grieving she'd done had been in private. Will never once saw her cry.

Before he realized it, he was on his own street, bypassing Henry's altogether. Another plan he'd have to put off till the morning.

• • •

"Where have you been?" Hannah scolded when Will stepped inside. "It's going on eight o'clock and a soldier's been here looking for you. They're calling in the cadet corps from all the schools. You're to report to City Hall. *Immediately*, he said, and that was two hours ago. But first—" She stopped and gave him a hug. "I looked for your mum on the Commons and in Victoria General, but she wasn't there. I'm sorry, love."

Will nodded. "Tomorrow we'll try again. Right now I need to get changed."

"Don't you go rushing off! You've been working all day and into the night and I can see you're worn out. And the things you've seen—no, I won't have it. You've been through enough. You don't realize you're in shock like everyone else."

"I'm not in shock, Hannah, and I have to go. As soon as I get changed, I'll be off. Did you polish my boots for me?" he teased.

"Will!" she shouted after him. "You're going to make yourself sick, and who's going to have to take care of you? Me, that's who! And you can polish your own darn boots!"

Within minutes Will was back, dressed in his cadet uniform. It was safe to say that nobody would fuss about his unpolished boots or brass buttons, so he would waste no time in doing either. He wrapped up some cheese and stuck it in his pocket. "For later," he said. "Could be they'll have news at City Hall about missing people. Wish me luck."

CHAPTER 17

Thursday, December 6, 1917
Evening

Livy heard a faint ringing and stirred. *It's the little one, Peter, and he's found a bell in the wreckage. He's ringing for help. I can see him behind the overturned bathtub.* She pushed herself up to reach him, only to realize that she'd been dreaming. She fell back into the eiderdown.

The ringing continued. It was the front doorbell. Was it Henry, calling on Will? Maybe it was Eliza. She didn't want to see Eliza. She would've been in school when the explosion happened and would want to describe every detail. But what had happened in the South End to Eliza and her classmates was nothing compared to what Livy had experienced. She couldn't begin to talk about it….

Sometime later, the ringing changed to a tap. Someone was at her bedroom door. "Clara!" Livy cried in alarm, remembering. She threw off the covers and jumped out of bed. "I'm sorry, I fell asleep and forgot—"

"No harm done," Hannah said, entering the room. "She was still asleep when I came home and that was hours ago. I shouldn't have gone off and left you, as tired as you were."

"Did you find…is there any news about Mum?" Livy held her breath, afraid of what the answer might be.

"No, love. I'm sorry. But it's early yet, and we won't stop looking. Meanwhile, there's someone here to see you."

Livy shook her head. "I can't…not Eliza."

"It's not Eliza. Come." Hannah held out her hand.

The last person Livy expected to see was Kathleen. Yet there she was, sitting at the kitchen table in one of Mum's dressing gowns, rocking Clara in her arms.

She sank into the chair next to Kathleen, stunned. "How…?"

Kathleen glanced at her with a haunted look in her eyes. A look that told Livy she couldn't talk about what happened any more than Livy could.

"She's in shock," Hannah said. She poured strong tea in a cup, stirred in a large spoonful of sugar, and passed it to Kathleen. "Drink this, Kay," she said. "I'll take Clara."

Kathleen did as she was told. Her movements were slow. Her eyes were vacant. A bandage covered one cheek. Her left hand was wrapped in gauze. When she raised the cup to her lips, her hand was shaking.

"Let me." Livy took the cup and held it to Kathleen's lips.

"She came to the door about an hour ago, when you were asleep," Hannah said. "Shaking like a leaf, black from head to toe, her clothing in tatters. I brought her inside and when she saw Clara, she fainted. How she survived, how she made it out of Richmond and all the way here…."

"Why here?"

"Habit, I suppose. Except for the last week or so, she's been coming here almost every day for the past year and a half. And since people were being told to leave the North End, she came south. She might have gone to the Commons first, maybe Camp Hill, to look for her brothers and her dad. We'll have to wait for her to tell us." She got up and poured more boiling water into the teapot.

"She was covered in soot and blood, same as you, when she got here. Had a shard of glass sticking out of her cheek. I pulled it out, washed her face, and put on the bandage. Her hand, the one that's wrapped up, was burned. She's got cuts on her legs as well. I put her in your mum's dressing gown—it's a bit too big but it'll do. We'll have to see what else we can find."

By now, Kathleen had finished her tea. She reached out for Clara, wrapped her arms around her, and kissed the top of her head. Other than that, she remained still.

"She and Clara can stay here," Livy said. "Mum wouldn't mind. Would she?" She rose from her chair, not waiting for an answer. They had three spare bedrooms on the second floor, plus the empty servants' rooms next to Hannah's on the third floor. They could take in all sorts of people needing shelter. "I'll make up the bed in the big room—Oh." Her face fell. "Will you show me how?"

"Sit down!" Hannah was as firm as she'd been earlier. "You've had a shock as well and I won't have you overdoing it."

"You said it was best to keep busy," Livy reminded her.

"Sometimes! And since when did you ever listen to me?"

"I had a nap like you said. Even though I didn't mean to."

"True, but you could break down and collapse any minute. And if that happens, you might not bounce back so quickly. So you're staying put. I'll teach you how to make a bed some other time. Besides, I've already made up the bed. Where else are they going to go?"

• • •

In a matter of hours, City Hall had become the gathering point for anyone offering assistance or dropping off donations. It was also the place where hundreds of people were coming to ask for food, clothing, blankets, and medical attention.

Officials had wasted no time in organizing the cadets into three groups. One to work with the medical committee at City Hall, another to deliver food baskets to the families who had requested them, and the third to act as messengers.

Will was assigned to the third group. For the next four hours he delivered messages to addresses in the North End—all handwritten, since the telephone and telegraph lines were down. It was tough going, stumbling around with a torch and looking for addresses that were often impossible to find. Whole streets were demolished and houses were still burning. He had to return a great many messages to City Hall, undelivered.

"I'll be back tomorrow," he told the officer in charge at the end of his shift. "As soon as I've gone to a few hospitals. My mum's missing."

"I'm sorry to hear it," the officer said. "Your mum comes first, of course, but try and get here as quick as you can. We need you. The lines could be up and running and there'll be a backlog of telegrams."

As chance would have it, Will was leaving City Hall when he bumped into Henry. "Am I glad to see you!" Will said, amazed that his friend was in his cadet uniform and showed no signs of injury. "I've been thinking of you—even looked for you at Camp Hill—but what happened? You were running down to the fire, last time I saw you."

"I never got there," Henry said. "Some luck, eh? I was off to the fire, like you said, but I got to thinking about Lewis and how he'd probably want to see it. So I turned around and ran home. I was there when the explosion happened. But Lewis...."

"He wasn't at home?" Will frowned.

Henry shook his head. "The thing is, we can't figure out where he might have gone. He wasn't at home, or at school, or on the way to school. But you know Lewis. He'll show up eventually. Like a dirty shirt, Mum says. Always around, whether you want him there or not." He gave a rueful laugh. "Just ask Livy."

Henry must have seen something in Will's face that prompted him to say, "What is it? Something happen?"

Will told him about Livy and his mother.

"No!" Henry looked shocked. "Livy was in Richmond? It's a wonder she's all right. And your mum—I'm sorry, I should've asked right away. She spends so much time in the North End, I should've—"

"You weren't to know." A thought came to him. "Is it possible that Lewis was following Livy this morning?"

"Oh, gosh. I hope not."

"I'll ask her, just in case. Are you going home now?"

"No, I'm working here all night. They put me with the medical committee 'cause I've got first aid, but mostly I'm running between here and Camp Hill and everywhere else with names and addresses of people needing a doctor. Trying to look for Lewis at the same time. I'll look for your mum, too."

Will nodded. "Thanks, pal. Might see you tomorrow. And I'll keep an eye out for Lewis."

He got home after midnight, glad to be out of the cold, the wind, and the snow that was now falling. The weather had changed for the worse.

As he was removing his boots, he noticed a note stuck to the banister. *Kathleen's here*, it said in Hannah's writing. *Be quiet when you come up the stairs.*

Will read the note a few times, trying to take it in. Maybe Hannah was right and he was in shock, or maybe he was too exhausted to think straight. But after such a day, he didn't know what surprised him more—the fact that Kathleen was there, or the fact that he really wasn't that surprised.

CHAPTER 18

Friday, December 7, 1917

"Who's calling at this hour?" Hannah grumbled. Someone was ringing the doorbell and it was not yet six in the morning. "I'll be some cross if they wake up the others. And if Norman starts yapping—"

"Sit down," Will said as Hannah rose from her chair. "I'll get it. It could be important." He hurried down the hall and opened the door, prepared for the worst.

Standing on the porch was Henry, his cadet uniform covered with snow.

"Come in,"Will said."Want some breakfast? It's snowing like the dickens out there. What's happened? Do they want me at City Hall right away?" His questions skirted around the one question he had in mind but was afraid to ask.

"Can't stay, but thanks," Henry said. "I'm on my way home. Just wanted to stop and tell you that I saw your mum, and she's alive."

"Oh!" Will gasped. "Thank god! Where? When?"

"An hour or so after you left last night. I was taking a message to Camp Hill and saw her being brought in on a stretcher. I heard her before I saw her, actually—you know how loud she can be sometimes. She was calling for a nurse."

"Did you talk to her? How did she seem?"

"Her face is pretty beat up and her eyes…." He winced. "They hadn't been treated. I said hello to her but she didn't respond, not even when I told her who I was. I don't think she could see me, Will. And she didn't recognize my name."

"Did they put her in a room? Where can I find her?"

"She was in the main hall, still on a stretcher, when I left. I reckon she's in a bed by now, hopefully with her eyes bandaged. I've learned that the eye injuries get seen to first."

Will ran a hand across his brow. "I'm so relieved. Just knowing that she's alive. I can't thank you enough for stopping by."

"I heard the news!" Hannah rushed down the hall the instant Henry had gone and gave Will a hug. "Wait till we tell Livy!"

"It's not entirely good news," Will cautioned. "Henry doesn't think she can see."

"Never mind that! We know where she is and that's good enough for now."

Will had already put on his boots and was buttoning his coat. "When Livy gets up, tell her I've gone to Camp Hill to see Mum. Better not tell her about the eyes until I learn more."

Will arrived at the hospital in good time, in spite of the falling snow. Given the early hour, it wasn't that crowded and, after finding a nurse willing to answer his questions, he located the ward where many of those with eye injuries were being kept. It took him a few moments to determine which brown-haired patient was his mother, as everyone's eyes were bandaged. Some had their entire heads swathed in bandages.

He moved from bed to bed, saying her name quietly so as not to disturb the others. "Mrs. Schneider? Mum, it's me."

Finally, from the bed next to the window, he heard, "Will! Oh, thank goodness!"

He went to her, relieved but shocked at her condition. She was alive, she was in hospital, she wasn't as seriously injured as some, but there was no hiding the fact that she was in a bad way. Her face was swollen and bruised, marked by numerous cuts, and a bloodstained bandage covered her eyes. Her hands were crisscrossed with cuts.

"Mum, I can't tell you how relieved I am. Are you…how are you?" Will sat on the edge of the iron bed and took her hand. Now that he'd found her, he didn't know where to start.

"Will, can you get me another blanket?" She spoke more slowly than usual, but her voice was strong. "The nurse won't come—do you think it's because of my German name? I'm freezing. I might as well be outside. Why is it so cold?"

"It's cold because the windows were blown out. There was an explosion—"

"Where am I?" she interrupted. "I know it's a hospital because they did something to my eyes but it's not Victoria General. Is it? I should be in Victoria General."

"All the hospitals are full. People are waiting outside to get in. Mum, you're in Camp Hill—"

"No! It's not finished, and it's for soldiers with shell shock. You know, mental problems. I don't belong here. Tell them, Will. And the noise! People coming and going, all night long, asking where's this person or that person. I can't see anything, but I can hear. It's bedlam. And there's never a nurse, not when you need one. At least I'm in a private room, and it's a bit quieter now. But wouldn't you think they'd close the door? You have to tell them."

A private room? He took a deep breath. "Don't you know what happened?"

"Someone brought me here, that's all I know. Must've done, because I woke up on this board—surely it can't be a bed—and my eyes were covered in bandages. I heard the Germans dropped a bomb and the whole city is gone. But that can't be right. And the pain! It's a stabbing behind my eyes, like daggers of glass. Will, you've got to ask them for morphine. And when's your father coming? It's taking him long enough."

Will took a sharp intake of breath. *Doesn't she remember?* This was something he hadn't expected, and he had no idea how to handle it. Not recognizing Henry's name was one thing, but to think Dad was coming? *Best tell her what happened, and save the rest for later.*

He told her about the explosion and how he'd found Livy. "She's fine," he said. "And Hannah's fine. And the house—"

"Why is it so cold?"

"Because all the windows were blown out," he told her again. "Everywhere in the city, even at home...." He paused, seeing that she'd sunk down in her bed and no longer seemed to be listening. He wondered if she'd heard or understood anything he'd said about the explosion. "Try to get some sleep, Mum," he said. "I'll be back tomorrow with Livy."

He gave her a tender pat on the head and left the room, hoping she'd be less confused after she'd had more rest.

Already there were more searchers in the crowded hospital than there'd been when Will had arrived, as well as more wounded needing attention. Nurses, doctors, and volunteers were setting about their tasks in a hurried but efficient manner, and Will couldn't help but be impressed by their calmness. He stopped a passing doctor, apologized for interrupting his work, and asked about the morphine. "My mum's in a lot of pain," he explained, instantly regretting both his words and his request. What patient wasn't in pain? And who was he, to ask for special privileges?

"There's no more morphine," the doctor said bluntly. "And we've run out of anaesthetics. Anyone needing surgery has to bear it without. Sorry, son. Now if you'll excuse me…."

Without anaesthetics? Will shuddered. He would have liked to ask the doctor about his mother's condition, but that would have to wait. What mattered the most was that she was alive and safe.

CHAPTER 19

Friday, December 7, 1917

"Can't we go now, Will?" It was mid-morning, and Livy was becoming more and more impatient.

"There's over a foot of snow already and it's still coming down," her brother said. "It's going to be hard to walk. Took me long enough, and the weather wasn't as bad as this. Are you sure you're up to it?"

"Yes, for the hundredth time," Livy said, putting on her coat and reaching for her hat. For the past hour, from the moment he'd come home, Will had been trying to discourage her from going. Mum needed her rest, he'd said. She was confused and in pain. Seeing her in such a state would only make Livy upset. "Honestly, I'll be fine," she insisted. "I need to see her..." Her voice began to tremble. "Please, Will."

He sighed. "Let's go, then. I was hoping Kathleen would be up by now, but since she's not...." He gave a disappointed shrug. "Did she say anything about what happened?"

"Not a word," Hannah said, coming down the hall to see them off. "And don't you go asking, not till she's more like herself. As for you, Livy, don't stay out too long. You're foolish to be going out at all, but nobody listens to me."

The temperature had dropped to well below freezing. Livy's first breath caused a spasm in her lungs that made her cough. The coughing hurt her ribs. Had she cracked a rib without knowing? She pulled her scarf up to cover her mouth and nose.

"Okay?" Will had to shout to make himself heard above the wind.

She nodded. Will was right. The walk would be difficult, especially as she was feeling more pain than she had the day before. Every bone and muscle in her body ached. It was a wonder she could move at all.

The falling snow, heavy and wet, clung to their clothes and eyelids. The wind whipped into their faces and forced them to walk with heads lowered or turned aside. Will went ahead, leaving tracks for Livy to step into.

She pictured a snow-covered Richmond and wondered how the rescuers were managing. The snow would be like concrete. Digging through to the wreckage would be an ordeal in itself, let alone finding bodies. There'd be no hope of survivors after a night of freezing temperatures.

The streets leading to Camp Hill were clogged with snow and abandoned vehicles. Some had broken down or been stuck in drifts. Many were unable to make it up the hills. Even horse-drawn sleighs were having difficulty.

The weather had not discouraged people from turning up at the hospital. Livy gasped at the sight of the large crowd gathered at the entrance. She took Will's hand, bracing herself as he led her inside.

"Watch your step," he said.

Slowly they edged their way past, around, and over the carpet of mattresses and people. Snow melted and dripped from their boots and clothing, soaking mattresses and adding to the misery of the wounded. Bare stretches of floor were slippery with melting snow.

It was taking so much of Livy's concentration to watch her step that she managed to avoid looking at anyone directly. But suddenly she stopped, her breath caught in her throat.

A girl her own age sat hunched and shivering against the wall. Her clothing, the little of it that remained on her body, was in tatters. Parts of her face and neck were burned, and one of her legs was in an odd position. The girl must have felt someone staring for, at that moment, she looked up, caught Livy's eye, and stared back. Almost as if she were daring Livy to do or say something. As if she were thinking, *What right have you to be here, staring at me?*

Livy looked away, ashamed. "I can't, Will," she said. "You were right. I can't do this."

He squeezed her hand. "I'll walk you home. All right?"

She nodded, took a few steps, and stopped. "No, I better see it through. I've come this far."

She carried on, wondering why the girl had made her feel uncomfortable. Not guilty, exactly, but *wrong*. Given what had happened, she should not be walking down the hospital corridor with only a bandage on her forehead to show that she, too, was a victim. It wasn't enough. She should be seriously wounded, sitting on a mattress beside the girl or lying in a morgue. The least she could do was acknowledge the suffering around her and not turn away.

• • •

"In here," Will said when they reached the ward. "Mum's over by the window."

Livy's heart sank. Mum looked frail and helpless, not at all like the mother she knew. Her skin was smudged a sickly grey, probably from someone's attempts to wash off the black soot. Her wounds were red and bluish-black and swollen. Livy dreaded to think what her eyes looked like beneath the bandage.

"I'm back, Mum," Will said. "I've brought Livy."

"Olivia? Come closer."

Livy stepped up and took Mum's hand.

"Not so tight!" she cried. "It hurts."

"Sorry," Livy said, seeing the cuts on her mother's hand. "I should've known."

"You don't sound like Olivia. Your voice is croaky. Lean over so I can feel your face."

Livy tried not to wince as her mother's fingers explored her face, touching her cheeks, chin, and nose, stopping at the thick bandage on her forehead. "What's this?"

"A bandage, Mum. You sent me to Kathleen's." She began to tremble. "The house collapsed. I was buried...."

Her mother moaned loudly, giving no indication that she'd heard or understood what Livy had been saying. She turned her head to the side of the bed where Will was standing. "Have you heard from your father? The Germans dropped a bomb. He'll be in danger."

Livy frowned. "Dad's not—"

"There wasn't a bomb," Will cut in. He looked at Livy, a finger to his lips, telling her not to say any more.

"You need to warn him before he's arrested," Mum went on. "Will, do you hear?"

"Yes, but Mum, there was an explosion—"

"Where am I? What kind of a hospital is this? It's not Victoria General. Why am I not in the General?"

"I told you this morning, Mum." *Twice.* "There's no room in the other hospitals. You're lucky you're in a bed." He shook his head, exasperated. "Kathleen's safe. So is her little sister. They're staying with us."

"Oh, no. We can't have those people living in our house."

"They have nowhere else to go," Livy said.

"They have to leave! I need the house kept tidy for my meetings. The Red Cross is coming on Monday and the Temperance Union—what day is it now? Have you told the other ladies where I am? They can't do it on their own. Oh, dear lord!" She raised her hands to the bandages covering her eyes. "Will, you must find a doctor and tell him to take these off. I can't see!" Her voice rose in panic. "I need to get back to work!"

She was struggling to push herself up when a young woman with a trolley entered the ward. "There, there, Mrs. Schneider," she said. "Lie down now. I'm Frances, and I'm going to check your wounds for splinters. Just in case we missed some the first time around."

Will and Livy watched as the woman took a pair of tweezers from the trolley and set to work removing slivers of glass or wood from the cuts. Their mother bore it in silence, though her face showed that she was in pain.

"Are you a nurse?" Will asked.

She shook her head. "I'm a student at the university, second year biology. I came here yesterday and volunteered. Someone sent me to the kitchen to wash surgical instruments, and while I was doing that, a doctor came in and asked if I had a steady hand. I said yes, so he gave me this job." She spoke up and turned to her patient: "We're almost through, Mrs. Schneider. You're doing fine."

"I should be at the General," she muttered. "They have proper nurses there."

Frances was struggling to remove a sliver of metal from a cut on her patient's hand. "That was a nasty one," she said, dropping it onto her tray. "When that ship blew up, every microscopic thread of her came down on something or somebody. I'm picking out a lot of metal as well as glass. Then I scrub the wounds so they don't get infected. I try to get to as many patients as I can but it's overwhelming."

She dropped some blue tablets of antiseptic into a bowl of hot water and began to scrub tar and soot from the wounds. "If you're wondering when the bandages can come off her eyes, that's up to a doctor to say. There! We're all done, Mrs. Schneider. Someone will be along to wash away the rest of the soot, and someone else will bring a hot brick for your bed. There's a blizzard outside. Did you know?"

"No one tells me anything," she grumbled.

"You know that's not true," Frances said, and moved off to the next patient.

She'd no sooner left than a nurse came in, her face haggard and her eyes red from exhaustion. A volunteer accompanied her, holding a lantern to help her see.

The nurse nodded to Will and Livy, and leaned over her patient to change the dressings on her eyes. Livy looked away.

"Do you know what happened to her eyes?" Will said.

"Flying glass, I suppose. She was already bandaged up when I got here."

"When can she come home?"

"We won't know until Dr. Cox has a look. He's an eye doctor from Truro, the only one we have at the moment. Arrived last night around six o'clock and hasn't stopped working since. Most patients, as soon as they're treated, out they go. The serious eye injuries will be here for a while."

Will lowered his voice. "Is Mum's injury serious? Could she lose an eye?"

"That's up to the doctor to say."

He nodded. They stood in silence as the wind shrieked between the boards on the windows, blowing in snow. "We're leaving, Mum," he said. "We've got to get home before the blizzard gets worse."

She hadn't spoken while the nurse had been changing her dressings, nor had she reacted to their conversation. Now their mother said, "Will, why hasn't your father come to see me? Tell him I miss him. And next time you come, bring Olivia."

Livy gasped. "Mum…?"

"Come on," Will said, and led his sister out of the room.

"Who did she think I was?" Livy said. "Is she losing her mind?"

He patted her shoulder. "She'll come around. She doesn't know what she's saying."

On the way home, Livy tried not to worry about her mother's confusion. Instead, she thought about the girl she'd seen in the corridor and tried to figure out why that particular girl had caught her attention. There'd been something about her, even before she'd caught Livy's eye, but once Livy had seen her eyes and her unnerving stare—*Jane*, she suddenly realized. The tough girl from the North End who'd offered to help her find Russell Street. The blast had ripped apart her braids and the black rain had covered her red hair, but nothing had changed that frank and open gaze. Had Jane recognized her? Had she wondered why Livy had gotten off so lightly?

I'll call you Liv, she'd said. A moment before the sound of the collision had drawn her away.

• • •

"Mum's still confused," Will said when they returned from the hospital.

"She'll get over it," Hannah said matter-of-factly after Will had explained. "It's hard for the moment, but don't you worry. Just give her time."

How much time? Will wondered. He rummaged through his pocket and drew out a folded broadsheet. "Take a look at this," he said, handing it to her. "The *Herald* is already printing newspapers. We passed the building on the way home. Every window was blown out and the printing press was filled with broken glass. So they printed it by hand."

Hannah unfolded the sheet and began to read.

HALIFAX WRECKED: More Than One Thousand Killed In This City, Many Thousands Are Injured And Homeless.

She looked at Will, her eyes wide. "Dear god. I never imagined…."

"You can't, unless you see it for yourself," he said. "What happened in the South End is nothing. The *Herald* says one thousand killed, but it's bound to be more." He shook his head, his face grave.

After a moment he went to the counter and pulled a leg from one of the freshly roasted chickens set to cool on the counter.

"Those chickens aren't for you!" Hannah said, swatting him with her wooden spoon. "They're a food donation to take to City Hall. For people who've lost everything!"

"Sorry," he said, attempting to put it back.

"Oh, all right," she relented. "You needn't look so hard done by. I'll keep this one for us."

"You're swell, Hannah. Thanks. Where's Kathleen? And Clara?"

"Resting in their room. The dog, too, needless to say."

"We told Mum about them staying here. Whether or not she'll remember is another story."

"Hmm. I'll bet that went over well. Please tell me you didn't mention the dog."

"Heck, no." He finished the chicken leg, sat down with a bowl of soup, and skimmed over the paper, paying close attention to the list of the missing and the dead. There was no one matching the name Grant or any other name that he recognized. Except for one. "You know that Lewis is missing?" he asked Hannah.

"Henry's brother? The one who's sweet on Livy?"

"What did you say about Lewis?" Livy had changed out of her damp clothing and taken a place at the kitchen table.

"He's missing. Henry told me last night. It's a mystery where he ended up."

Livy looked stricken. "He was following me. You know what he's like. He wanted to know where I was going. He was excited because he'd seen the ships going towards each other and he thought there might be a collision and did I want to go and see—"

"Calm down, Livy. You're starting to shake."

"And I told him to get lost. I didn't mean it. I didn't think he'd go missing. Stop looking at me like that. It wasn't my fault." It was the most she'd spoken since the explosion. Her throat still felt raw and she couldn't control the shaking.

"Of course it wasn't," Will said, surprised by her outburst. "Did I say it was?"

"No, but I feel that it was."

He sighed, not knowing what to say. He looked again at the lists in the paper. "Kathleen will need to add her dad and brother to the missing."

"Two brothers," Livy said.

"Only one now," came a quiet voice.

"Kathleen?" Livy turned to see her standing listlessly in the doorway. Her eyes looked clearer than they had the day before, but her voice was flat and full of despair.

"Tommy's gone. I saw his body. So now there's just Peter and my dad, Joe. Dad worked at the rail yard so I don't have much hope."

Hannah put her arms around Kathleen and led her into the room. "We don't give up hope until we know for sure."

"Peter and Joseph Grant. I'll add those names for you," Will said as he got up. "Soon as I put on my uniform I'm going back to City Hall. The *Herald* is close by."

Kathleen nodded. "Clara's asleep upstairs. Hannah, if you could mind her. . . ." She lowered her voice to a whisper. "I have to go to the morgue."

"You're not going alone," said Hannah, removing her apron. "Livy won't mind watching Clara when she wakes up. Will you, love? Don't worry about Lewis. There's nothing you could have done. Nothing. And don't worry about your mum. I'll stop by the hospital and see if I can—oh, I don't know what. Say something to jog her memory."

• • •

Five hours later they were having tea in the parlour, waiting for Will to return from City Hall.

"Livy," Hannah said, "I hate to tell you, but my visit with your mum didn't go as planned. She was asleep when I got there and when I said, 'Fiona, it's me, Hannah,' she said, 'Go away, I'm not the one you're looking for,' and went back to sleep. It's early yet, though. We have to give her time."

Livy was some fed up with hearing that she had to give things time, but said nothing. She took a bite of sponge cake and was knitting her third balaclava when Will came home.

"You won't believe this," he said excitedly. "The rescuers were searching the ruins of a house when they found a baby, about the same age as Clara, and she was alive—after twenty-six hours!"

"No!" Hannah was dumbstruck. "She survived over-night, in that frigid weather?"

"Yes! They found her in the ash pan under the kitchen stove. The blast must have thrown her there, and since the ashes were still warm, that's what kept her from freezing. So don't give up hope, Kathleen. Miracles do happen—Oh...." He went quiet, remembering that she had gone to the morgue and that, for her, the possibility of a miracle might be over.

She held up the small grey bag resting on her lap and said quietly, "All that's left of Tommy is in here. A blue shirt, short grey pants, two marbles, and a penknife that he wasn't supposed to have. Dad and Peter weren't at the morgue. So, yes. There's hope."

CHAPTER 20

Saturday, December 8, 1917

"Wait!" Hannah called from the front door. "I've got another box."

"Don't rush," Will said. "The walkway's still slippery." He and Livy had cleared the steps and shovelled snow from the walk earlier that morning, anticipating several trips back and forth to the motorcar.

"Is there room for another box?" Livy asked. The back seat was already bulging with boxes of warm clothing and blankets, as well as crates of food.

"Don't fret," Hannah said. "This one's light. You can put it on your lap." She handed her the box along with a shopping list. "Some of the grocers are open, so if you're close to one, and you think you can manage—"

"I'm fine," Livy said.

"Well only if you're sure. And if you do make it to the grocer's, check for broken glass before you buy anything. The last thing we need is splinters in our cheese."

"*Ibby! Me too!*" Clara was toddling towards them, wearing a coat over her flannel nightdress, an oversize hat, and slippers on her feet.

"You rascal!" Hannah scooped her up and kissed her cheek. "You'll catch your death!"

"No! Me too!" she protested, squirming in Hannah's arms.

"Another time, Clara," Will said. He helped Livy get seated with the box and started up the engine.

Although snowplows had been out on most of the main roads, their progress was slow. Every few yards they had to get out to clear away branches and other obstacles.

"Stay inside," Will told Livy during one such stop. "Won't take me a minute."

He thinks I'm doing too much, she thought, but didn't argue. Instead, she used the time to look inside the box. Hannah hadn't mentioned that many of the items had belonged to Livy's dad. Socks, ties, shirts, vests—"Oh!" She gave a small cry, overcome by the sight of a blue woollen scarf. It had been her first attempt at knitting and she'd given it to him for Christmas, the first year of the war. *It's long enough for the two of us!* he'd teased, laughing as he wrapped it around both their necks with enough left over for the rest of the family, including Hannah.

Livy smiled, remembering. Her tension on the needles hadn't been right and the scarf had stretched beyond a reasonable length. Dad hadn't minded.

She held it to her face, breathing in the familiar smells of sea salt, pine needles, pipe tobacco, and peppermints. Smells that brought him back more sharply than any memory or photograph. The wool felt soft against her cheeks.

She wrapped it four times around her neck and let the ends hang down the front of her coat.

"Remember this?" she asked when Will came back to the car.

"The ever-stretching scarf!" He grinned. "How could I forget?"

"I'm going to keep it. Is that all right?"

"Of course," he said, and squeezed her hand.

• • •

City Hall was bustling. Cadets and other volunteers ran in and out, calling out messages or picking up requests for coal, blankets, and food. At the same time, there was a steady stream of people bringing in donations.

"I'll stay here and do a shift," Will said to Livy after they'd unloaded the car. "You sure you're up to the shopping? You know what Hannah said. And can you make it home on your own?"

"I'm fine. Stop fussing!" It was starting to annoy her. It was as if he'd taken on the role of both their parents—the one who was gone, and the one who might as well be. Hannah was just as bad.

Instantly she felt ashamed. If Will was acting like a parent, it wasn't by choice. He was missing Dad and Mum as much as she was. As for Hannah, of course she'd be concerned. She'd taken care of Livy since the day she was born.

She apologized to Will and left to carry out her errands. At least she hadn't let on about her sore muscles.

The wind was strong, the sun was breaking through the clouds, and there was no falling snow. With the welcome change in the weather and no telling how long it would last, there were more people on the streets than she'd expected. Many showed the signs of survivors. Arms in slings, faces and hands dotted with bandages. Some, like Livy, bore blue scars, a reminder of the black rain that had become embedded in wounds.

Apart from the people, the downtown area had the look of a ghost town. Banks were open, as were several stores, but all the windows were boarded up. The clocks in every building showed five minutes after nine.

There wasn't much in the grocery store. Except for canned goods, all the food had been thrown out because of glass damage. Hannah would be disappointed but, for now, two cans of peas would have to do.

Later that day, she and Will paid another visit to Camp Hill. Moving along the crowded corridor was as gruelling as it had been the day before but, in some areas, things were improving. Volunteers were going from room to room and recording the names, addresses, and injuries of the patients. Lists were being posted outside each door so that patients wouldn't be disturbed by people coming in to look for missing friends or family.

Livy and Will read the lists that had been completed but found no Lewis Fraser or Joseph or Peter Grant among the names. Livy hadn't seen Jane in the corridor and was unexpectedly disappointed when she didn't see the name *Jane* listed anywhere.

Mum looked a little better, now that more of the black soot had been scrubbed off. The dressings on her eyes had been changed again that morning, and she told them that Dr. Cox would be examining her eyes before the end of the day. She still complained about the stabbing pain behind her right eye. "They won't do a thing about it, Will. They're giving me nothing for the pain, nothing! The sooner I move to the General, the better. Do you know when, Will? I've been waiting for a week!"

"Only two days," Livy said.

"And as for seeing the doctor," she went on as if Livy hadn't spoken, "why am I at the bottom of the list? He should have seen me right away. Doesn't he know who I am?"

"He's from Truro," said Livy.

"Any doctor worth his salt should know about his patients, for goodness sake. Ask him, Will. Ask him why it's taking so long for him to examine my eyes."

"It's probably a good sign," Will said. "It probably means that your injuries aren't that serious."

"Well you tell this Dr. Cox that there's going to be trouble when Ernst gets here—when did your father say he was coming? It's been weeks!"

"Sure, Mum. I'll tell him." He gave Livy a just-bear-with-it-for-now look.

Livy bit her tongue. *Mum wouldn't "bear with it" if it were the other way around.* She wished she hadn't come.

"I've been working at City Hall with other cadets," Will was saying. "Right now I'm delivering messages but I'm going to be driving soon. Taking the wounded to and from hospitals or dressing stations. I've offered our car. The city needs cars—"

"*What*?" Mum almost bolted from the bed. "You can't!"

"Sorry, but if I hadn't volunteered the car, the soldiers would have commandeered it. They're doing that to anyone they find driving. This way I can drive it myself. They don't care that I'm not quite old enough."

"It's almost brand new," she cried. "You'll get blood all over it."

Will's jaw tightened. "Yes, probably. And mud and soot and gosh knows what else. But the car's being put to good use and it can be cleaned."

"Your father will have something to say about that."

"He'd do the same thing," Livy muttered.

"And he won't be pleased when I tell him about people living in our house," their mum continued. "Have you got rid of them yet?"

"No!" Livy retorted, unable to bear it any longer. "They're staying, and so is their dog! And we have tea in the parlour whenever we want to! And I'm Livy, in case you'd like to say hello!" She stormed off, leaving Will to handle their mother.

Outside the ward, she sank to the floor and hugged her knees, waiting for the shaking to stop. Shoulders, arms, fingers, legs, her whole body trembled. She regretted her outburst. Poor Mum, it wasn't her fault. But the anger! How could she be in pain and still have the energy to be angry? And not to be able to see.... *That's why she's confused and angry*, Livy thought. *When her eyes are fixed, she'll feel better and think clearly. But what if she doesn't? What if her eyes can't be fixed?* These were questions she couldn't begin to answer.

CHAPTER 21

Sunday, December 9, 1917

Livy woke with a start, her heart pounding in her ears. A flash of light broke through a gap in her curtains. A thundering boom shook the house. She leapt up and scrambled under her bed, trembling with dread. *Another explosion! Please, God, keep the house safe.* She held her breath, waiting for the roof to collapse onto the attic and the floor above her head, everything falling on top of her, pinning her down—

Then, a different sound. A pelting against the window so violent it threatened to break the glass. *Rain!* She hugged herself with relief and crawled out from under her bed to look.

Lightning lit up the streets. A wind with the force of a hurricane snapped branches and swept up debris, hurling it down the street. Another fork of lightning. Another clap of thunder. Shrieks from down the hall. Was it Clara or Kathleen?

Livy ran to their room and found them wrapped in each other's arms, shaking. "A storm," she said. Another roll of thunder made her jump and clap her hands over her ears.

"Stay with us," Kathleen said.

Livy joined them under the quilt, pulling it over her head to block out the sounds of the storm. Beside her, Kathleen was humming softly to Clara. A lullaby. The most beautiful sound Livy had heard in a long time.

• • •

It was still raining late the next morning when Livy left for Camp Hill. The heavy rain made walking difficult, but that wasn't the worst part. The temperature had risen as dramatically as it had fallen the day before, leaving a mess of slush from the melting snow. The slush was blocking street drains and, in some places, flooding the roads.

Livy leapt over a deep puddle, relieved that she didn't have to fight a freezing wind and blinding snow. But how many weather disasters could they take on top of everything else? How would people with damaged houses manage if they were flooded? She put the matter aside for the time being and concentrated on the task ahead.

Will had asked if she'd be able to go to the hospital on her own, as he'd promised to put in a full day of driving for City Hall. She'd agreed. Partly because she owed it to Will, partly because she regretted her outburst the day before, and partly because there was the chance that this day might be better.

Still, she dreaded another visit. The searchers, the injured, the gloomy atmosphere, the smell of blood and antiseptic—she could cope with all of that. Coping with Mum was a different story.

She slowed her pace and went out of her way to avoid puddles in order to prolong the journey. She was in no hurry to face her mother. *What do I say to her? How do I make her understand that I'm Livy? How do I tell her that Dad won't visit because he's gone?*

Livy's mum had always been critical of her. Dad had said that it was because she and her mother were too much alike. Will, on the other hand, could do no wrong. *She'll spend the whole time asking why Will hasn't come—if she knows he's my brother, that is. And when I remind her that he's a volunteer driver, she'll complain about him using our car. If I tell her about Kathleen and Clara she'll complain about them living in our house and say they'd better be helping Hannah and earning their keep. If I tell her about the relief committees that are out helping people, she'll say they won't do it properly. She'll grumble and complain about the nurses and doctors and the food and the noise and the cold and the whole time, she won't even know who I am. I'll stay for one minute. That's all. Maybe five. Definitely no more than ten.*

The crowds clustered around the entrance were as frantic as they'd been on her previous visit. Even more so, since soldiers were now guarding the entrance and letting only a few in at a time. Livy ducked under a couple of arms and slipped in without being noticed.

She went up to the second floor and paused for a moment before moving on to her mother's ward. Something had changed. She'd sensed it downstairs as well. There were just as many patients waiting for beds, but there were also more nurses and doctors. She remembered what Will had said the night before about relief workers. There'd been a steady stream arriving from other provinces, and he'd heard that an entire trainload of doctors, nurses, and medical supplies had arrived from Boston.

Hopeful that her mum might have received some good news from one of the new doctors, and might even be ready to come home, Livy entered the ward. She frowned, thinking that she'd entered the wrong one by mistake. No, it was the right ward. She recognized some of the patients. Every bed was occupied. But the lady in the bed next to the window was not her mother.

Livy's heart plummeted. A sick feeling rose into her throat. She grabbed a nurse's elbow to stop her from leaving the room. "What's happened? Where's Mrs. Schneider, my mum? Has she died?" She clapped her hand to her mouth as if to push back the possibility. If she'd hurried to the hospital instead of dawdling, if she'd arrived sooner, if she hadn't had those thoughts about not wanting to see her….

"Mrs. Schneider?" the nurse said. "She was moved last night, to Bellevue Hospital."

"Bellevue? Where's that?"

"It's in the Officer's Club, the three-storey building at the corner of Queen and Spring Garden Roads. The medical team from Boston was looking to set up a temporary hospital and they picked that building. Worked on it all day yesterday and by midnight it was ready to take patients."

"Why's she there? She'll hate it!" Livy tried to keep her voice down but she was becoming more and more agitated. Her mother, in a makeshift hospital that they'd only just opened? "She can't stay there!"

"Come with me." The nurse put an arm around Livy's shoulders and led her down the corridor to another room. A screen had been placed across the open door. "This is the operating room," she said. "Dr. Cox set it up for the eye cases. He examined your mother's eyes yesterday evening, and told her she had to have both eyes removed. She'd have none of it. She screamed and kicked at anyone who tried to approach her."

"No! That can't be my mum!"

"It's hysteria," the nurse said.

"She's a lady!" Livy went on. "She doesn't make a fuss. She'd do what the doctor said!"

"It got so bad yesterday that we were afraid she would harm herself or somebody else. And Dr. Cox—he'd been operating straight for over thirty hours—he decided your mum would be better off elsewhere." The nurse patted Livy's shoulder kindly. "Try not to worry. Your mum had calmed down by the time they took her to Bellevue. The medical supplies have been pouring in and we were able to give her morphine."

Not worry? "She's losing both her eyes? Are you sure?"

"That's what the doctor said. Actually, it may have been done already."

Mum, blind? How will she manage? Livy's head felt woozy, her knees weak. She leaned against the doorjamb to steady herself. "But her eyes were bandaged. We thought she'd been treated. A nurse told us she wouldn't lose an eye and now you're saying—"

"Calm down, dear. That might've been the case if they'd removed all the glass. But they didn't. There were hundreds of eye cases, they had to be treated right away, there weren't enough doctors, everyone was rushed and exhausted...there wasn't even time to sterilize. Mistakes happen. Your mum was complaining of pain. Screaming, in fact—"

"A stabbing behind her eye," Livy remembered.

"That's right," said the nurse. "When Dr. Cox examined her eyes, he found more slivers of glass and a splinter of metal. The nurse changing the dressing should have noticed, but with the poor lighting and everything...I'm so sorry, dear." She tucked a loose strand of hair under her cap. "I've got to get back to work. Can you find your way to Bellevue? You can't miss it. There's an American flag hanging out over the street."

Livy gave her a blank look.

"Maybe you should wait and have your brother go with you," the nurse said. "Will, is it? You mum cried out for him several times. And Ernst? She kept asking why he hadn't come. Is he another brother?"

"My dad," she said, "but he's gone."

Livy turned and made her way back through the hospital, overwhelmed. Her mum, losing her sight. Acting out of character. Kicking and screaming in a public place. Crying out for Will and Dad but not for Livy.

• • •

The rain had stopped by the time she reached Bellevue Hospital. The Stars and Stripes hanging over the sidewalk made her feel nervous, as if she were about to enter foreign territory. Not knowing the condition her mother would be in made her even more anxious. *What if she doesn't know me? What if she doesn't want to see me?* Her heart dropped. *See me? She won't ever be able to* see *me again.*

It's no wonder she cried out for Dad and Will, Livy thought. *She always depended on Dad. Now she relies on Will. I'm the one who can't do anything right.*

Saddened and crushed by everything the nurse had told her, Livy tried to summon the courage to enter the hospital. But after several minutes, she turned around and made her way home.

• • •

Will got home from his shift at City Hall much later than expected, and wanted nothing more than to go upstairs to bed. He hadn't even begun to remove his coat, however, when Livy appeared. He was surprised, given the lateness of the hour, but one look at her distraught face told him that something was wrong. After hearing about her visit to the hospital and what she had learned, he was out the door and on his way to Bellevue.

He didn't blame his sister for not going inside to see their mum. Not knowing what to expect, especially after Mum's out-of-character behavior at Camp Hill, would make anyone nervous. He felt the same way. Mum, losing both her eyes? How could that be? No wonder she'd been hysterical.

He found her without difficulty. Her eyes were covered with fresh bandages and she was sleeping soundly, like most of the patients in the ward. He didn't want to wake her.

"Excuse me, young man." A soft voice made him start, and he turned to see a young nurse approaching. "I'm sorry," she said, "but visiting hours are over. These patients need their rest."

"I was leaving anyway," Will whispered. "She's my mum. How is she?"

"Her condition is stable," the nurse said, walking him towards the exit. "We'll know tomorrow. Today was… difficult. She was in surgery early this morning and she had a terrible time afterwards because of the ether. Patients are often very sick when it wears off. She was in a lot of pain, too, until we gave her some morphine, and that helped her sleep. She does have a strong heartbeat. Something tells me she's a fighter."

Will managed a smile. "That's true enough." He couldn't bring himself to ask about her eyes. What was the point?

"Good night then," the nurse said when they reached the door.

Before stepping outside, Will asked the nurse if she was from Boston.

She chuckled. "Did my accent give me away? It's a bit different from yours, but not by much."

"Thanks for coming," he said as he opened the door. "I can't tell you…."

"We're neighbours," she said. "Halifax would do the same for us if the tables were turned."

"Even so…thank you."

CHAPTER 22

Monday, December 10, 1917

"Have you seen this?" Hannah handed Will the morning *Herald*. "Police have rounded up some Germans. And the electricity's back on. Did you notice?"

He clenched his teeth and nodded. *It put me in a good mood until I saw this*, he thought angrily. He tossed the paper aside with disgust. "Sixteen Germans who registered with the military at the start of the war. *Honest* men. If they were spies, or if they planned an attack, would they have registered? I'm fed up with all of this." It was hard enough having to cope with his mother's blindness, let alone the anti-German sentiment that pervaded the city.

He said goodbye and got ready to go outside. The weather had changed yet again. Although there were still banks of snow, freezing temperatures had turned the puddles of slush and rain-soaked streets into sheets of ice. Driving to City Hall in such conditions was a chance he didn't want to take, so he decided to walk. *Storm off* was more like it. A good way to get rid of his anger, as long as he didn't slip and break his neck.

He was halfway to City Hall when he heard a voice shout, "Hey, Fritz! You happy now?"

A packed snowball flew past, narrowly missing his head.

"What were you doing at Mackey's house the other night? Congratulating him on causing the explosion?"

Will recognized the husky voice. *Percy George.*

Another snowball hit him in the back of his neck.

"Turn around, Kaiser *Vilhelm*!"

Will stood still, listening as Percy and another boy stomped up behind him. He waited until they were close enough for him to hear their breath. Then, without warning, he scooped up an icy wad of snow, whirled around, and smashed it into Percy's face. He hadn't planned to hit the eye but he did, and he pressed in the gravelly shards of ice crystals, pressed in deep, digging in and shouting, "My mother's lost both her eyes, my sister was buried, my best friend's brother is missing, I've been digging bodies out from the wreckage and driving injured people to hospitals and you—you lazy, cowardly pig—what have you done?

Nothing! And you dare to say I'm to blame? Who have you lost? Have you even been to the North End?"

By now he had both hands around Percy's throat and was shaking him with pent-up rage. "Don't you ever, *ever*, bother me again."

He released his hands and gave a violent shove, causing Percy to lose his balance and fall flat on his back in the snow.

Percy's companion gaped.

"What are you staring at?" Will snapped. "Go on, help him up. You're his friend, aren't you?"

"Not really." The boy shrugged and walked away.

Will watched Percy struggle to get up. He felt a certain satisfaction, seeing the lout regain his footing only to slip and fall again. The more he struggled, the slicker the snow became. "You're pathetic," Will scoffed.

He carried on, still fuming. When was it going to end? The rumour in Richmond about a second explosion had proven false, as had the one about the Germans being behind the explosion. But while the local papers had dropped the first rumour, they kept harping on about the second. So did everyone else. Maybe it wasn't the Germans *directly*, they argued. But the *Mont Blanc* had been loaded with explosives meant for the war. The German Kaiser had started the war. And since there was no way that people could punish *him*, they had to find someone at home.

It had been bad enough before the explosion, but now! People with German surnames were being yelled at in the street, or had rocks thrown at them, or their homes vandalized. The other day, a German shopkeeper who'd lived in Halifax for twenty years had installed a new pane of glass only to find it smashed the next morning, and all the items he'd put on display in the window, stolen. Will hated to think what his dad might have had to endure.

He stopped at an intersection and took several deep breaths to slow the surge of adrenaline. He hadn't been so heated up in a long time.

After a few more breaths, he continued. He'd no sooner started to feel calmer when it began to snow. *Not again!* He kicked at a pile of snow and cursed as he entered City Hall, feeling as fed up and angry as when he'd left home.

His task for the day was to match undelivered telegrams to the names of people who were in hospitals or private homes. Once he found a match, he had to deliver the telegram to the person in question. It was a rewarding job, as most people were happy to hear from friends or family from away. But as the day progressed, the job became daunting.

By noon, the morning's snowfall had turned into a blizzard even fiercer than the one they'd had on Friday. By late afternoon over five inches had fallen. Will had to plow through knee-high drifts in some places to reach his destination. It would be some job clearing the streets when this storm was finished, what with five more inches on top of packed snow and frozen slush.

Try as he might, Will couldn't shake Percy's taunts from his mind, especially the one about Captain Mackey. And it wasn't just Percy pointing the finger. When they weren't blaming the Germans, newspapers like the *Herald* had been questioning the pilot's role in the explosion and suggesting that he was somehow to blame. *They'll probably make him the scapegoat,* Will reckoned. *They don't care that the collision wasn't his fault.*

By the time Will was on his way home, three things had happened to lift his spirits. He'd managed to locate over two-dozen names and deliver telegrams to each and every person. One was a telegram addressed to Joseph Grant on Russell Street, from a Louise Grant in Vancouver, B. C. Kathleen would be pleased when Will gave it to her.

The second good thing was that the blizzard had subsided to a few gentle flakes, eventually easing off to nothing at all. For the first time in days, Will walked home under a clear sky.

The third good thing was that he'd decided to write a letter to Captain Mackey. It was a small gesture, and probably wouldn't amount to anything, but Will knew he'd feel better knowing he'd at least done something.

As soon as he got home, he sat down with pen and paper and began to write. He told Captain Mackey that he'd seen the events leading up to the collision. He'd recorded them in his notebook, making it clear that the *Mont Blanc* had come into the harbour on the correct side, and if anyone was to blame it was the *Imo.* He ended his letter by saying how sorry he was that the newspapers were blaming Captain Mackey, and that he hoped the captain would not become the scapegoat.

Letter finished, he put it in an envelope. He'd deliver it to the pilot himself, right after dinner.

Next, he gave Kathleen the telegram. "From Aunt Louise," she said, and almost smiled. "My dad's only sister. She had five brothers, but Dad was her favourite. She told me once that he could always make her laugh. She'll be shattered when she hears that he—" Her voice broke.

"You don't know for sure," Will said. "There's still hope, remember?"

• • •

After delivering his letter to Captain Mackey, Will walked over to Bellevue Hospital to visit his mother. When he reached her ward, he was surprised to see that only the right eye was covered with a bandage. The left eye was uncovered, but extremely red and swollen. He winced, imagining how painful it must be.

"Slowly, Mrs. Schneider." A nurse was sitting beside her, holding a glass of water while her patient drank through a straw. "Tiny sips, that's the way...almost done." She turned to Will as he approached. "You must be Will. She thought you might be coming."

"I came last night but she was asleep. How is she?"

"Much better," the nurse said, smiling. "This is the first time she's been able to hold down a sip of water. She still can't eat, but maybe tomorrow."

He wanted to ask about the eye that wasn't bandaged, but the nurse was moving off to another patient.

"Will, is that you? Come closer."

"It's me all right. I hear you've had a rough time."

"I can't eat without vomiting, but it's probably just as well. Nurse said I'd be tasting nothing but ether for days. At least I can see a bit with my left eye."

"You can?"

"Only close up. Everything else is a blur."

"But a nurse at Camp Hill told Livy that both of your eyes had to be removed."

"I know, it's been terribly confusing. One minute they say one thing, the next it's something else. The doctor at Camp Hill said that both eyes were severely damaged and had to be removed. Apparently I put up such a fuss that they moved me here. Poor Dr. Cox from Truro. I'm afraid I might have kicked him."

"The nurse told Livy that, too."

"Oh, dear. That's the last thing she needed to hear. Anyway, the Boston doctor had a look and said yes, the right eye had to go, but the left eye could be saved. And once the swelling goes down, my vision will improve. So that's how it is. I won't be totally blind."

"Does your right eye hurt? I mean—"

"The eye that isn't?" She gave a loud sigh. "It's just a socket now, they tell me. Hurts like the dickens, to be honest. Like there's a two-ton weight pressing on it. Don't tell Olivia. She'll be upset. So will Hannah." She groaned and put a hand to her throat. "Hurts to talk. Another side effect of the ether."

"Just nod, then. Is your stomach still queasy? I've got to give Livy and Hannah a full report."

"Not so bad," she whispered. "Go home, Will. Get some sleep. You look exhausted."

The night was cold and still, the sky bright with stars. Thinking of his mum and what she'd said before he left, Will felt unexpectedly moved. Not only because she could *see* that he was exhausted—that alone was a breakthrough—but also because she'd shown her concern. She'd sounded more like the mother she'd been before his dad had died.

By the time he got home he was feeling less exhausted and more hopeful than he'd been in a long time. If Livy was asleep, he'd wake her and share the good news. He gave a dry laugh. A week ago they would have been devastated at the thought of their mother losing one eye. And now, not losing both was almost a cause for celebration.

CHAPTER 23

Tuesday, December 11, 1917

"Good gracious, Livy. Where are you off to?" Hannah said, seeing Livy in her coat and boots. "The wind's a right fury!"

"*Wite fooey*!" Clara echoed. She'd taken to imitating whatever anyone said, and the resulting babble of sounds was often amusing, if impossible to understand.

Livy laughed. "Stop picking on me. The wind's not that bad." She was in good spirits after Will's news about their mother, though he'd advised her to wait another day before visiting. "It's not raining or snowing and the sun's out. So I'm going for a walk up Citadel Hill."

"Arf, arf!" Norman barked at the word *walk*.

"You want to come too?" Livy gave him a pat. "All right, but only if it's okay with Clara."

"*Wite fooey! Itadel me too!*" Clara babbled, struggling with her boots.

"Nap time for you, Clara," said Hannah. "No ifs, ands, or buts."

"Mind if I come?"

Livy turned to see Kathleen coming down the stairs. "Of course not," she said. "Whenever you're ready."

The two girls walked without speaking, but that was no surprise. Kathleen had been quiet since the day she'd arrived, except when she was playing with Clara.

Livy picked up a stick and threw it for Norman to fetch. The puppy was growing at a fearsome rate. "Eating us out of house and home," Hannah complained, but she was besotted with the dog as well as with Clara. Livy couldn't help but wonder what would happen when her mum came home. A toddler and a puppy, while coping with one eye? At least Norman was house-trained.

Hannah was fond of Kathleen, too. Kay, as she called her. Watching them prepare meals together or do other household chores—those that Kay could manage with her burned hand—made Livy realize how close the two were. She'd never noticed before. She'd never noticed *anything* before. Hannah treated Kathleen like a daughter. They didn't talk—well, *Hannah* talked—but they didn't seem to need words to communicate. They understood each other. No wonder Kathleen had shown up at their door.

Livy wasn't bothered. A few months ago she might have been jealous, but not now. And she wasn't bothered by Kathleen's silence. She'd been fairly quiet herself. Hannah and Will kept asking when she was going to call on Eliza or her other school friends, but she wasn't ready. When Eliza stopped by on Sunday afternoon, Livy had told Hannah to say she was "indisposed." The truth was, she felt more comfortable walking in silence with Kathleen than spending time with Eliza. She didn't know what had happened to Kathleen on that terrible day. The fact that Kathleen had *been* there, and suffered, was enough.

Livy wrestled the stick away from Norman and tossed it again. "Go get it!"

At the top of Citadel Hill, they stood and looked to the north. "Will saw everything from here," Livy said.

Kathleen said nothing.

The devastated area stretched before them, blanketed by the previous day's snow. The blackened, skeletal remains of the trees and buildings, and the battered ships in the harbour looked painfully grim in contrast to the blue sky and sunshine.

Like everyone else in the city, Livy wondered who was to blame for the explosion. At least one thing was certain. "It wasn't a German bomb," she said out loud. The more often she said it, the more reassured she felt. "The ship, the *Mont Blanc*, was carrying explosives. A 'floating bomb,' Will said."

She wasn't sure how much Kathleen knew or didn't know about the explosion, but now that Livy had started to talk, she couldn't stop. "The *Mont Blanc* blew to smithereens, every bit of her, except for a part of the bow that got grounded on the sand. Will told me. He went down to the harbour to look. All the explosives, all the metal, every little bit blew up and rained down in splinters and black tar. Mum got metal in her face and her eye, not only glass. We don't know where she was when it happened. She hasn't told us.

"I was at your house, in the kitchen. You told me to take my coat off but I didn't. I wasn't planning to stay more than a minute. I was feeding Clara and, just like that, we were buried. If it wasn't for Norman barking and running around the wreckage...." Livy lifted her shoulders in a shrug. "We hardly got any injuries. I don't know how we survived."

Norman was yapping at Livy's feet, wanting her to throw the stick. She picked it up and let him chase her for a while before throwing it and rejoining Kathleen.

"I was on my way downstairs."

The voice made Livy start. She turned to Kathleen but Kathleen's gaze remained fixed on the ruins.

"I'd gone up to get the boys and for a minute I watched the fire with them. Then I lost my patience. I said, you need your breakfast now or you'll be late for school. But they wouldn't budge. All right then, I said, if you get the strap for being late it'll be your own fault and I won't be sorry. That's what I told them. Then I left to go downstairs.

"Next thing I knew I was lying on the ground and the black rain was soaking into my clothes and my skin. My hand was red and raw from a burn and my arm was at a crazy angle so I knew I was hurt but I didn't feel any pain. I got up and I didn't know where I was, it was like another country. It was my neighbourhood, my home, but nothing was familiar. Not even the people. I should have recognized somebody but I didn't. Not until I saw a soldier carrying Tommy. I called his name but he didn't move. I told the soldier he was my brother and I asked him, Are you taking him to hospital? But the soldier said no, he was sorry, he was going to the morgue. He put him in an open wagon filled with people. No one was moving."

She stopped for a moment, her voice breaking. "I wanted to go with him and hold him...." She took a deep breath before continuing. "I lost myself after that. I should've stayed and looked for Peter and Clara and my dad, but at the time I wasn't thinking. It was like my mind had gone away. All I could do was follow the wagon. A man stopped me and looked at my arm. Dislocated, I think he said. He moved it somehow so it was the right way around. It should've hurt, I should've been screaming, but I didn't feel a thing.

"There were soldiers on horseback shouting orders. I didn't understand what they were saying. I only saw panic in people's faces and in the horses' eyes and I let myself be swept along."

A cloud covered the sun. Livy shivered and shoved her hands deep into her pockets for more warmth. She felt a hard, smooth object and took it out to see what it was. "Oh my gosh," she said. "I'd forgotten."

Kathleen looked at the object. "A piano key. My mother used to play by ear. Popular songs and folk songs, you know. My dad would sing along and if he didn't know all the words he'd make them up. Then the boys and I would join in and we'd end up laughing to bits." She smiled, but her eyes were bright with tears. "After she died, none of us had the heart for it."

Livy handed her the key. "It's yours. It was lying beside me in the wreckage and it…." She paused to collect her thoughts. "It helped me, somehow."

Kathleen nodded with understanding. "The smallest things can do that." She closed her eyes and clutched the key to her heart, as if remembering all that it symbolized.

She reached out her other hand and Livy took it, holding it tightly as they walked home.

CHAPTER 24

Wednesday, December 12, 1917

"Mum, it's me, Livy. Are you awake?"

Her mother turned her head and opened her eye, moaning with pain. Her face and neck were bruised and nicked with cuts and the skin around her left eye was discoloured and puffy. The right eye was still bandaged.

"Olivia!" Her lips curved in a smile. "Will said you were coming this morning."

She knows who I am! Livy's heart surged with relief. "How are you, Mum?"

"Better. It doesn't hurt so much to talk and I can eat a bit." She paused. "I saw your father last night."

Livy was stumped. *Dad, here?* If he showed up at all it would be at their house, not Bellevue Hospital. The building hadn't even been a hospital at the time of his accident, and it certainly hadn't been flying the American flag. Her mother could not possibly have seen him.

"It was a dream," Mum said, as if reading Livy's thoughts. "It wouldn't be possible otherwise. Mind you, here in Halifax the impossible has happened." She paused, mulling over the words before continuing. "He was removing my bandages. He said, 'Fiona, everything will be fine. You'll see things clearly now.' What do you suppose he meant? I wanted to ask, but he'd gone. I felt much calmer afterwards."

"I've seen him, too," Livy said. "I saw his face when I was being rescued. And when I was leaving the North End, I saw him in the crowd. I tried to catch up but I couldn't move fast enough." The memory made her heart race and her body tremble. She loosened her scarf as a surge of heat rushed through her veins. *Say something, Mum. Say anything to show that you're listening.*

Silence.

Livy began to pick fuzz balls off the scarf and braced herself for the usual scolding.

The silence continued.

When she could stand it no longer, she looked up and saw tears spilling from her mum's eye. "Mum?" she said, alarmed. "Are you all right?"

"Will told me what you went through," she said. "How you were buried.... I'm sorry. I never should have sent you there." Her shoulders shook with sobs.

Livy swallowed hard. Too overcome to speak, she leaned forward and used the end of the scarf to dab away her mother's tears.

She was about to sit back when Mum clasped her hand and said, "Wait. Is that the scarf you knit for your dad? It has his smell."

Livy hesitated, fearful that her mother might be cross. "It was in a box of donations but I couldn't give it away."

"I'm glad." Mum smiled. "Thank you for wearing it, Livy. Thank you for coming."

• • •

Livy walked briskly, her spirits high. The change in her mother's mood was as dramatic as the change in the weather. It could turn back in a minute but, for now, it was a promising sign. *She knew me! And for the first time I can remember, she called me Livy.*

If the nurse hadn't shooed her away so that her mother could sleep, Livy would have stayed longer. There were so many things she wanted to say, now that Mum was—what? Better? She'd lost an eye, for heaven's sake. But she was remembering things and she wasn't cranky. The very fact that Mum was *there*, and not rushing off to do something or be somewhere, was a gift. It was an odd way to think, given the circumstances, but there it was.

Maybe it was a good thing that she'd been shooed away, Livy thought. She might have said something that made her mother angry—

A loud clanging brought her up short. *Get down!* A voice shouted in her head. *Get down!* But there was nowhere to go. Her legs wouldn't move. She sank to her knees in the snow and covered her head with her hands, shaking with fear, waiting for the blast....

"Hey, are you all right? Let me help you up. Did you fall?"

She blinked hard, took a few deep breaths, and looked at the man who had helped her. "Thanks," she said. "I slipped on some ice." Easier to lie than to admit she'd been spooked by what she now realized was the clanging of a trolley bell. The trolleys, it seemed, were back up and running.

She thanked him again and carried on, still trembling.

• • •

That afternoon, Will burst into the kitchen with a letter in his hand and an incredulous look on his face. "They want me to testify!"

Livy looked up from the castle of blocks she was building with Clara. "Testify about what?"

"*Esteye wat?*" repeated Clara.

"The investigation into the collision. It starts tomorrow. They want me there on Friday."

"Why *you*?" said Hannah. "And who's *they*?"

"A man called Mr. Mellish." He held up the letter that had been delivered moments before. "He's a lawyer for the *Mont Blanc*. I never thought it would come to this. All I did was write to Captain Mackey. He must have—"

"You didn't!" Hannah gaped. "Don't tell me you're supporting that man after what he did."

"Will, how could you?" Livy looked shocked.

"I saw what happened," said Will. "Of course I support him. He must have shown my letter to the lawyer, because Mr. Mellish says I shouldn't hesitate about testifying. He says it'll take courage, and he'll understand if I say no, but—"

"Well you're not going to do it," Hannah said. "Your mother won't have it."

"Please don't," said Livy. "You're asking for trouble. It's bad enough, people thinking it was the Germans."

"That's exactly why I *am* going to do it. You know what it's like to be accused of something you didn't do. Think of how brave Dad was, standing up to all those false rumours."

"Leave Dad out of it!" Livy abandoned the castle of blocks and stormed from the room.

"*Ibby mad*," said Clara.

"You're making a mistake," Hannah said.

"*Me mistay*?"

"No, Clara. Not you. Will. Someone has to be responsible and it might as well be Mackey."

"*Captain* Mackey. And he's *not* responsible." Will left the room in pursuit of his sister.

"Go away," Livy said from behind her bedroom door. "I'm not talking to you until you make sense."

"Fine," he said. A pause. "I'm going to see Mum and tell her. Want to come?"

"And hear her yell at you, for the first time ever? I'd like that very much but not today. Go away."

• • •

Will was surprised to find his mother out of bed and walking down the corridor, with the help of a cane.

"Doctor's orders," she said, after Will voiced his concern. "He said it was time to get moving and I agreed. My legs were wobbly at first but they're getting stronger. I'll take a rest now that you're here."

Will helped her back to her bed, asking, "How's your vision? Your eye still looks sore."

"I haven't bumped into anything yet. Feels strange having one side blocked when I'm moving around. Like a horse with partial blinders. I'll get a patch in a few days and then I should be ready to go home. Now, what have you got there?" She indicated the letter in Will's hand.

Will read her the letter. For several moments afterwards, she remained silent.

Is she confused about what it means? Will wondered. *Or is she simply mulling it over*? He hoped she wasn't sinking back into the confused state she'd been in at Camp Hill. Or building up to an angry outburst.

When she spoke, her voice was calm and matter-of-fact. "Mr. Mellish is right. It will take courage to stand in front of a courtroom and answer questions. There'll be questions from both sides and they might be tough on you. They'll try to confuse you."

"I'm not worried," said Will. "I know what I saw."

"Yes…but there are others to consider. The courtroom will be full of people who are suffering, and they'll want someone to answer for it. You can expect a lot of bad feeling. Are you prepared for that?"

"I don't know, to be honest," he said. "I hope so."

"I don't agree with your doing this. I'd rather you didn't, for your own sake. But I understand why you want to, and I have to say I'm proud of you. Your father would be too."

"Thanks, Mum." Will swallowed the lump in his throat and changed the conversation to how she was feeling.

Much better, she told him. "I'll have one good eye," she said. "I'm lucky."

• • •

Livy had calmed down by the time Will got home. "I'm not talking to you, but I have to say one thing," she said, arriving at his bedroom door.

"I'm listening," said Will.

"Everyone says it was the *Mont Blanc*'s fault. Well, Mr. Mackey knew that the ship was full of explosives. Didn't he? And he *lives* here. So why didn't he just move to the other side of the harbour? Why was he so stubborn about the right of way when he knew what could happen?"

Will couldn't argue. Everything she said was true. But still, the blame could not be laid on one man. "He was probably expecting the *Imo* to move over," he said. "Anyway, how do you think Captain Mackey feels? All those people killed, including some of his friends. Some of his own family got hurt. A whole quarter of his city was demolished. He hardly did it on purpose. It was an accident."

"It was more than that!" she said hotly. "How do you think Kathleen will feel when she finds out you're standing up for Mackey?"

He started to speak but she cut him off. "Go away. I don't want to hear anymore."

• • •

Later that day, as Will was finishing his driving shift at City Hall, he ran into Henry.

"Will!" Henry said, grinning. "I've been looking for you. Lewis is in Camp Hill Hospital. He's in rough shape and won't be out for another month at the earliest, but he's alive and we know where to find him."

"Gosh, Henry! That's wonderful news. Your family must be relieved. I've got some news too." He told Henry about the letter from Mr. Mellish. "Do you want to testify? You were with me, and saw what I saw. How about it?"

"Not on your life," Henry said. "Besides, they'll have enough witnesses. Probably more than enough. Why don't you leave it?"

Will said he wouldn't consider it.

"Are you sure?" Henry said. "You might have been wrong about the whistles. Have you thought of that?"

"*What*?" Will stared at him in disbelief.

"You said there was only one blast from the *Mont Blanc*," Henry went on. "But I remember hearing two. So the *Imo* was expecting the *Mont Blanc* to cross—"

"You're wrong!"

"And the *Imo* gave two blasts because she agreed."

"Henry, how can you say that? You were right beside me!"

"Yeah, but the thing is…I'm not sure anymore. There's so much talk, and the newspapers—"

"Stop reading the papers! They're already against Captain Mackey and the inquiry hasn't even started. Do you think that's fair? It's obvious they think he's to blame. For all I know, the other lawyers and the judge think the same."

"So why bother being a witness?"

"Ohh!" Will threw up his hands in exasperation.

"Sorry, pal. My mind's on my work here at City Hall, and on my brother. He's in bad shape, like I said, and what happened that day…things aren't so clear to me anymore."

• • •

Will met Kathleen as he was walking home. She'd started volunteering at Camp Hill two afternoons a week, helping to feed patients, and was waiting to cross the street when he caught up to her.

"How are things at the hospital?" he asked.

"Busy," she said. "How's your mum?"

"Much better, thanks."

They walked for a block in silence, their footsteps crunching on the snow. She'd been out with Clara when the letter had arrived, and all day Will had been wondering if anyone had told her. He wanted her to know but, at the same time, he was afraid that her reaction might be similar to Hannah's. Finally he broke the silence. "I suppose you heard about the inquiry, and that I'm going to testify."

"Hannah told me."

"Well, I just want to tell you I'm sorry."

"Why?"

"Well, first they blame the Germans. And when they find out it wasn't the Germans, they look for someone else. Captain Mackey's an easy target."

"Actually," Kathleen said, "I was asking why you're sorry, not why you're testifying. You're doing what you think is right, so there's nothing to be sorry for. Least of all on my account."

"Oh." Will was taken aback.

Another silence. When they reached the end of the next block, she turned to him and added, "But thanks all the same."

CHAPTER 25

Thursday, December 13, 1917

The inquiry into the collision of the *Mont Blanc* and the *Imo* was being called the Wreck Commission, and it was attracting a lot of attention.

A large crowd was already waiting at the County Courthouse when Will arrived early the next morning. There were reporters from various newspapers as well as interested civilians, many bearing the scars of the explosion. At the appointed time, the doors were opened and everyone filed inside.

The room was like a cavern, dank, dark, and gloomy, with a ceiling over twenty feet high. The windows were boarded up and, since the power lines were still down in some places, the only light came from two oil lamps. There was no heat. With temperatures near to freezing, it was bitterly cold.

Hannah had urged Will (though grudgingly) to dress warmly, and he had followed her advice. Woollen long johns, a flannel shirt, a heavy sweater, a winter coat, a cashmere muffler wrapped around his neck, a fur hat—and he was still cold.

In the dim light he thought he recognized a couple of newspaper reporters sitting at the back. He found a seat behind them and took out his notebook. *Wreck Commission, Day 1, December 13, 1917*, he wrote. Exactly one week since the explosion.

At the front of the room, a man stood at what looked like a pulpit on a raised platform. Men in naval uniforms sat on one side of him. Important-looking men who might have been government officials sat on the other side.

Will tapped the shoulder of the man seated in front of him and asked about the person at the pulpit.

"That's Judge Drysdale of the Supreme Court of Nova Scotia," the man said, adding, "You're a bit young to be here, aren't you?"

"I'm old enough to want to know what's going on," Will replied. "And when I find out, I'm going to write an article about it."

"Aha! My future competition! You aiming to work for the *Herald* or the *Chronicle* one day?"

"No, I'm going to be a pilot like Captain Mackey. Right now I'm the editor of my school newspaper. I write a column on shipping news."

"You don't say! Are kids interested in that?" He looked skeptical.

"Not always," Will admitted. "At least they weren't before. They will be now. I saw the collision, you know. I'm going to be called as a witness tomorrow."

"Well, well. You don't say."

Will thought he detected a note of admiration in the reporter's voice. He was about to tell him more when the man said, "Here we go," and turned to face the front.

The judge was rising to his feet. He called the courthouse to order and waited for the talking to stop. Then he called the first witness, Captain Le Medec, the French captain of the *Mont Blanc*.

It wasn't long before Will's head started to ache.

Mr. Burchell, the lawyer for the *Imo*, fired questions at such a rapid speed it was all Will could do not to run out in frustration. It didn't help that the questions put to Captain Le Medec, as well as his answers, had to go through a translator. The poor lighting didn't help Will's headache either. He could hardly see the page let alone what he'd written.

Back and forth it went. Questions and answers in English and French. *How many whistles? Who signalled first? Who was on the right? Who was on the left?*

As the morning wore on, the confusion became greater. The lawyers weren't mariners and made mistakes with the terms. *Tiller? Wheel? Rudder? Helm?*

The questioning finally moved on to the deadly cargo the ship was carrying. Had the ship been inspected by the examining officer? Had he known what the ship was carrying? Yes and yes. The examining officer was told, "We're all explosives." So why didn't you fly a red flag? Because the red flag only had to be shown if explosives were being *handled* on board. The crew of the *Mont Blanc* wasn't handling the explosives. They were only *carrying* them.

Mr. Burchell then moved on to what happened after the collision. He asked Captain Le Medec why he hadn't warned people after the crew had abandoned the ship.

The captain said that they had tried. There were other ships in the harbour and his crew had waved and yelled to any sailors or officers who were close enough to hear.

That's right, Will remembered. Though he'd been too far away to hear, he had seen the crew frantically waving their arms. But if the crew had been yelling—and he didn't doubt it for a minute—it would have been in French. Would anyone have understood? Had Captain Mackey yelled a warning in English?

At last Mr. Burchell stopped his questioning. In his final comments, he accused the *Mont Blanc*'s crew of being selfish, the way they'd jumped ship and fled. He said they hadn't given a thought to anyone but themselves.

• • •

That evening, Will heard a knock on his bedroom door and opened it to Livy. Surprised, as she'd been avoiding him, he said quickly, "Before you get after me again, I have news about Lewis. He's at Camp Hill Hospital."

"Oh, that's wonderful! How is he?"

"He'll be there for a while but he'll pull through. Now, what do you want?"

The news about Lewis had thrown her. But only for a moment. "I don't like what you're doing," she said. "But Mum thinks it's all right and Dad…well, here." She held out the scarf. "Take some of Dad with you tomorrow. For good luck."

He took the scarf, deeply touched. "Gosh, Livy…."

She didn't wait to hear what he had to say. "Just remember it's not for keeps."

Sometime after that, Will heard another knock. "Change your mind already?" He got up from his desk, picked up the scarf to return to his sister, and went to the door.

"Hannah!" he said.

She glared. "Don't think for a minute I've changed my mind, you traitor, because that's not going to happen. I'd just as soon have you freeze in that courthouse, but if you go and catch a chill we both know who'll have to look after you. So take this."

Will recognized it right away. "Dad's sailing sweater," he said. "I thought you and Mum gave away all his clothes."

"Not quite all. I put some aside for you. Had I known what you'd be up to, I wouldn't have bothered. Now, you see those stitches?" She pointed to the complex patterns in the wool. "They're traditional in the part of Ireland my dad came from. They're meant to bring good luck and protection to whoever's wearing the sweater. I'll never forgive myself for not insisting your dad wear it that day, but never mind, you wear it and make sure those hoity-toity lawyers don't make a fool of you."

"Thanks, Hannah. You're swell."

He held out his arms to hug her but she slapped them away. "None of that! I'm still furious."

With that, she turned smartly on her heel and went upstairs to her room.

CHAPTER 26

Friday, December 14, 1917

What was I thinking? Is it too late to back out?

Will squirmed in his seat as the questions continued to plague him. His head ached, his stomach was grumbling, and his legs were twitching. After two hours of waiting, he still hadn't given his testimony.

Am I really doing the right thing? Yes, he was certain. But after seeing the *Imo*'s lawyer in action, he wasn't sure he still wanted to. Especially since he was starting to doubt what he had seen and heard on the morning of December the sixth.

He couldn't get Henry's remarks out of his mind. What if the *Mont Blanc* had given a two-whistle blast, and he had written "one" in his notebook by mistake? He and Henry had been excited by what was going on in the harbour. They'd been watching, talking, passing the binoculars back and forth—he could have been mistaken. As the minutes went by, he went over and over the sequence of events, hating the fact that he was beginning to question what he had absolutely believed to be true.

His head was throbbing in all directions at once. Front to back and side to side, the pain shooting down to his neck and up again, round and around until he thought he would be sick. *What am I doing here? One minute more, and if they don't call my name I'll get up and leave.....*

Another five minutes passed. *I have to leave now. If I get up on the stand and hesitate, if I stutter in front of all these people....*

Another five minutes. *It's not too late....*

But suddenly, it was. "We call to the witness stand, Wilhelm Ernst Schneider," came a booming voice from the front of the room.

He flinched, caught off guard by the use of his full name. Even to his ears, it sounded foreign. Shamefully, blatantly German. He wanted to shout, *No! It's just Will!* But the name was out and the spectators were reacting as expected, with loud intakes of breath, whispered comments, and hostile looks.

Ignore them, he told himself as he walked to the stand. *It's only a name. You have nothing to be ashamed of. It's Dad's name. Think about that and why you're here.* He smoothed down his sweater and adjusted the scarf. His dad had him well covered. He'd see this through.

Once Will was on the stand, he felt less anxious and his head stopped pounding. He answered Mr. Mellish's questions in a clear voice with no hesitations.

"Yes, sir. The *Mont Blanc* blew her whistle first."

"No, sir, it wasn't two blasts. It was one short blast, and the *Imo* responded with two short blasts."

"How can you be sure? Do you always remember things with such certainty?" Mr. Mellish asked.

"Yes, sir, I do when I write them down. I write for the school newspaper."

"No, sir. The *Imo* didn't change her course after that. She stayed where she was."

The questions and answers continued until Mr. Mellish thanked him and said he had nothing further.

Will smiled, confident that he'd done a good job and relieved that it was over. He was about to step down when Mr. Burchell came forward to begin his cross-examination.

Will's heart thudded. How could he have forgotten this part of the testimony?

"So, *Wilhelm Ernst Schneider*...." The lawyer spat out the words as if they were a bad taste in his mouth. "In your opinion, the *Mont Blanc* blew the first whistle. Is that correct?"

"Yes, sir, the first whistle came from the *Mont Blanc* and that meant she controlled the navigation."

"My word." He raised his eyebrows. "Impressive. However, you're not here to show off your maritime expertise, young man. Such as it is. Just answer the question."

Will felt his face redden. He loosened his scarf, uncomfortably hot. "Yes, sir. It was one whistle."

"That is your opinion?"

"No, sir. It's what I heard."

"You're saying it's *not* your opinion that the *Mont Blanc* blew one whistle?"

"Yes, sir. I mean, no, it's not an *opinion*. It's—"

"You're very young to appear as a witness. What are you, fourteen?"

Will bristled at the slight. "No, fifteen. I'll be sixteen in April."

"So you're fifteen. What qualifications do you have for appearing as a witness?"

"Qualifications?"

"Yes. Do you have experience as a sailor, for example?"

"No, but I was there. I saw what happened and I recorded it in my notebook."

"A *notebook*?"

"Yes sir, I write about shipping news for my school newspaper."

"Ah! Well that explains why you're such an expert." His tone was dismissive and condescending. "No further questions."

Will stepped down, his cheeks burning with humiliation. He took an end of the scarf to wipe the sweat from his face, lowering his head so as not to see the smirks, the glares, the shaking of heads. He grabbed his notebook and fled the courthouse, kicking himself for wasting the court's time, for upsetting Hannah and Livy, for letting Captain Mackey down. So much for doing the right thing. He'd accomplished absolutely nothing.

• • •

Will didn't talk about the inquiry over the weekend. When asked how things had gone during his testimony, he said, "Well enough," and left it at that. No one needed to know about the humiliation he'd suffered. They'd feel sorry for him and say, "I told you so." And Hannah, after she'd told him not to let the lawyers make a fool of him? Hah! He didn't want her to know how well *that* had turned out. Besides, what was the good of telling her? She and everyone else would read about it in the papers.

He braced himself for the remarks that might appear. How a fifteen-year-old "expert" with a German name had made a fool of himself in front of a packed courtroom. How a so-called "reporter"—and a German to boot—had twisted the facts in an attempt to save a pilot from the condemnation he deserved. Oh, yes, the *Herald* would have a grand time with his pathetic court appearance.

On Saturday, and again on Sunday, Will tried to get to the paper before anyone else so he could hide it if need be. But on both days, Livy beat him to it.

"I thought you gave your testimony on Friday," she said, after reading about the proceedings in Sunday's paper. "There's no mention of you at all. There wasn't in yesterday's paper, either."

"Really?" He took the paper, read the account, and saw that she was right. "Guess they didn't have enough space." He was relieved but, at the same time, unexpectedly disappointed. Had his eyewitness report counted for so little? Or were the reporters taking pity on him because of his age? He didn't know which was worse.

"Well, thank goodness for that," Hannah said. "Bad enough standing up for that monster in court, let alone having your name in print for all to see. You can get back to doing something useful now. Forget all that court nonsense. The sooner the schools open again, the better."

Will agreed. Nevertheless, he made it known that he planned to return to the courthouse on Monday.

"You gave your testimony already," Livy said. "Why are you going back?"

The last thing Will wanted to do was show his face at the courthouse, but he wasn't about to tell her that. "Mostly because I want to write about it for the school newspaper," he said. "And tomorrow's the day that Captain Mackey has to testify. I have to see how that goes."

"Everybody knows how that's going to go," said Hannah.

Will ignored her comment. He hated to admit that she was probably right.

There was another reason for going back. If he stayed away, the people who had ridiculed him or sneered at his name would have won. That was something his dad would never have let happen.

All weekend he'd been thinking about his dad and what he'd had to endure because of his German background. The loss of clients and friends. The name-calling. The vandalism to his office and to his sailboat. The invitations that had stopped coming—invitations to dinners and balls that Mum had looked forward to, like the ones held at Government House. The hurt he must have felt, knowing how his German name and accent had affected his family. Yet, in spite of everything, he'd never backed down. He'd carried on as always. And Will would do the same.

CHAPTER 27

Monday December 17, 1917

"Are you sure you're up to it?"

It was the day of the funeral for the unidentified dead, and Hannah had been asking Livy the same question all morning. "There'll be crowds of people and coffins—I don't want you getting upset."

Livy gritted her teeth and gave Hannah the same answer as always. "I'm fine. Stop fussing." She adjusted her black armband and stepped outside to wait for the others.

A few days earlier, Kathleen had had a private funeral for her brother Tommy. Hannah had paid for it, and Will and Livy had helped Kathleen dig the grave, using a pick and shovel to break the frozen ground. With hundreds of victims to be buried and few labourers available, many families were forced to do the same.

Kathleen had put off the funeral as long as she could, hoping that she'd have some news about her father or her brother Peter. She'd made daily trips to the morgue. She'd scoured the public notice boards and newspaper lists, praying to find some indication that they were alive somewhere, *anywhere*—in a hospital, shelter, private home, even in a different town. She'd looked for her own name as well as theirs, in case one or the other had posted a notice asking about her whereabouts. Her searches had turned up nothing.

"Dad and Peter might be among those buried today," she said as they were walking to the trolley stop. "Some of the remains were impossible to identify...nothing but bones and ashes. So they might be buried today," she repeated, "along with friends and neighbours, people I knew."

"*Papa? Peta?*" Clara had picked up on the words and was starting to cry.

"There, there, sweetheart," Kathleen said. "Look," she said, spotting the oncoming trolley, "we're going to take a trolley ride." She bounced Clara on her knee once they'd taken their seats, hoping to distract her.

Peter. Livy tried to put the boy out of her mind but he wouldn't go away. His face was in her waking thoughts and recurring nightmares. The same thoughts, the same nightmares. The feeling that Peter had been buried in the wreckage with her and Clara, in a different part of the house, under too much rubble for the rescuers to see. She'd felt the same about Kathleen and Tommy and had been proven wrong. But Peter...the little one who'd asked her name and invited her into his house, who'd revealed that his older brother was always getting into trouble. If they'd kept searching, if they'd searched more quickly and more thoroughly, if they hadn't fled the area with everyone else—they might have found him. Not necessarily alive, because he might have been killed by flying glass or by a heavy beam. But at least they would have found his body.

She'd had the dream the night before, and had cried out in panic, "Keep looking! Don't leave him behind!" She'd woken up shaking, struggling to breathe—

"Livy?"

She jumped.

"Sorry to startle you," Kathleen said, "but we're almost at our stop. Are you ready?"

Livy nodded.

The funeral was being held at Chebucto Road School—a regular school until the events of December the sixth turned its basement into a morgue. Livy hesitated at the sight of the crowd gathered there. Thousands of mourners, dressed in black or wearing black armbands, were lining up behind the picket fence that surrounded the schoolyard. Many were weeping into white handkerchiefs, trimmed in black.

"How are you feeling, love?" Hannah asked. "Not too late to go back if you're not up to it."

"I'm *fine*!" Livy snapped.

Her voice, unexpectedly loud and angry, startled Clara and caused bystanders to turn and stare. Hannah frowned with concern.

Livy lowered her head, embarrassed. Of course she was fine. Or *would* be if Hannah and Will stopped asking. It was nine days since the explosion. The wounds on her hands and forehead were still swollen and tender but they were healing. Her muscles were still sore and her body was covered in bruises, but each day showed progress. She was doing errands and helping out around the house—things she'd never done before. Her voice didn't sound croaky and her throat no longer felt as though it were being strangled.

Besides, saying "I'm fine" was easier than telling them about the nightmares. Or about the time she'd leapt out of bed and run downstairs to escape some unknown danger only to stop short, not knowing where she was or how she'd gotten there. Saying "I'm fine" was easier than telling them that loud, sudden noises filled her with panic, and made her look for somewhere she could take cover. And how could she explain that she was avoiding her friends because she wasn't sure how to talk to them anymore? If she told Will and Hannah all that, what could they do but tell her that she needed more time, and that sooner or later the feeling of terror would go away?

It would never go away. It was trapped inside her as surely as Kathleen's little brother had been trapped inside the burning house.

The service was about to begin. A band started to play the "Funeral March." One by one, the coffins were brought out of the morgue and placed in rows on the snow-trampled ground. Some were small and white. Others were long and dark, fitted with brass handles. All were covered with a sprig of flowers.

One by one, they were placed in front of the wooden platform where Catholic priests and Protestant ministers would be conducting the service. One by one, until there was a total of ninety-five coffins, some containing the remains of up to six people.

Clouds moved in and covered the sun as the Archbishop of Nova Scotia began to speak. "It is not by the hand of the Almighty these unfortunate human beings have suffered," he said, "but by the mistakes of others."

Livy heard a stirring behind her as someone spat out the name, "*Mackey*."

She shivered, saddened to hear the pilot's name being spoken at such a time and in such a hateful way. Will was right. The tragedy was too big for one person alone to be responsible.

At the end of the service, the coffins were loaded onto waiting trucks and flat wagons to be driven to Fairview Lawn Cemetery for burial. When there were no more trucks or wagons, passersby offered their sleighs.

• • •

Will attended the inquiry instead of going to the funeral. He was met with a few unfriendly looks but, for the most part, people seemed to have forgotten him. Reporters made no mention of his testimony. With Captain Francis Mackey about to take the stand, a fifteen-year-old schoolboy was of little interest.

The pilot's testimony began with a description of what happened on the harbour that fateful day. Everything he said matched what Will had witnessed. The *Mont Blanc* entering the harbour at half speed on the Dartmouth side, the *Imo* speeding towards her on the Halifax side. The ships taking action at the last minute and causing a collision. The collision causing the barrels of benzol to rupture. The friction of the steel hulls creating sparks. The sparks igniting the spilled benzol. And then, the fire.

Mr. Burchell attacked the pilot relentlessly, one question after another. Did you attempt to put out the fire? Why were you in such a hurry to abandon ship? Why didn't you warn people of the danger?

Captain Mackey answered the questions calmly and with confidence. Never once did he falter or struggle to remember. Never once did he backtrack and change an answer, in spite of the lawyer's goading. Yet to Will, it seemed as though the pilot's answers, though truthful and sound, were more or less ignored.

• • •

Livy was reading by the fire in the parlour when Will got home. Instead of reading a book or talking to her, he sat and glared at nothing, got up and paced the room, sat back down, and got up to pace again. After ten minutes of his distracting up and down nonsense she said, "What happened at the courthouse?"

"Don't ask!" he snapped. Then proceeded to tell her about Mr. Burchell's vicious attacks on Captain Mackey. "It's disgusting, how he gets away with it."

"He's acting for the other side," Livy pointed out. "Isn't he supposed to make Mr. Mackey look bad?"

"He doesn't have to make it personal. He actually read the names of men who were killed on the docks and on the ships, and asked Captain Mackey if he'd known them. What kind of question was that? Of course he knew them—and you can bet that Burchell knew it. One of those men was William Hayes, the pilot on board the *Imo*. He was a good friend of the captain's. Everybody knew that. He already felt terrible. Talk about rubbing salt in the wound."

He put another log on the fire and continued to pace the room. "And then, if that wasn't bad enough, Burchell brought up today's funeral. I swear he planned the whole thing. He waited until the exact minute when the funeral bells were ringing—the exact minute! And then, what does he do? He reminds Pilot Mackey that the bells were ringing for the victims who were never identified. As if he needed reminding. And you can bet that the whole courtroom was thinking what Burchell was thinking—*It's all your fault.* I swear I could—"

"Stop!" Hannah strode into the parlour, red-faced and clutching a wooden spoon. "We've had enough of this talk!"

"And then—"

"Enough! I'm warning you!" She shook the spoon at him and stomped out of the room.

"And then to top it all off," Will said, lowering his voice, "Burchell tries to get Captain Mackey to admit that he's been lying the whole time."

Livy was worn out with listening. "Hannah's right. We've had enough. It's over now, though. Isn't it? Captain Mackey has finished his testimony?"

"No," said Will, letting out a loud sigh, "he'll be back there tomorrow and so will I."

CHAPTER 28

Tuesday, December 18, 1917

Livy was home alone, finishing the last of the ten balaclavas she'd promised to knit for the Junior Red Cross. She was sitting by the kitchen stove, waiting for the kettle to boil so she could make some tea, when she heard a loud, rhythmic knocking on the back door.

Startled, she put down her knitting and tiptoed to a window. Tradesmen and delivery boys were the only ones who came to the back door, and Hannah hadn't told her to expect anyone.

Looking out, she saw a tall, ruddy-faced man dressed in a long brown overcoat, black trousers, and black-laced boots. A woollen muffler was wrapped around his neck and a heavy tweed cap sat low on his forehead. He looked respectable, but she wasn't about to open the door to find out.

She waited. Watched while he stood on the verandah, blowing on his bare hands, shifting from foot to foot, wincing now and then as if something was causing him pain. Occasionally, he'd tilt back his head to look at the upstairs windows.

He looked suspicious. Was he a burglar? Livy tightened her lips, determined to call the police if he didn't go away. Thank heavens the telephone lines had been repaired.

He knocked again. Whistled a tuneless something. *Not a burglar, then.* She didn't think a burglar would whistle.

He pushed back his cap, revealing a puffy blue scar that looked like railway tracks. It ran across his forehead and down his left cheek, narrowly missing his left eye.

An explosion victim. What's he doing here? Deciding that it wouldn't hurt to ask, Livy shouted, "I'm coming!"

To which he replied, "Kay! Is that you?"

His face fell when Livy opened the door.

"I'm sorry, lass. I didn't mean to disturb you. Is Kay here?"

"Kay? You mean Kathleen? Yes, she's here, but not here. I mean, not right this minute. But you're not—" She gasped. "You can't be—are you Mr. Grant?"

He smiled, revealing two missing front teeth. "I am, indeed. And you must be Livy. I've heard a lot about you and your brother, Will."

"Oh, my gosh!" Livy said excitedly. "Come in! Take off your coat and hat and sit down. I'll make us some tea." She ushered him into the kitchen, poured boiling water into the teapot, and placed two teacups on the table. "Mr. Grant! Oh, you can't imagine! Kathleen's been frantic! Searching everywhere, putting up notices, and when she sees that you're here, and alive—sorry, I have to stop and catch my breath."

He chuckled. A full-throated chuckle that reminded Livy so much of her father she felt her heart would burst.

"Sit down, lass. I'll fetch the teapot." He got up to do so, tripped over a castle of wooden blocks, and almost fell into the rocking horse.

"Careful," Livy said as he righted himself, "it's like a nursery in here."

As he took in the blocks, dolls, and spinning tops scattered around the room, his chin began to quiver.

Livy looked away, hoping he wouldn't start to cry.

He took out a handkerchief and blew his nose. "Kay never said there was a wee one in the house. You've got a sister?"

"Oh, no! All that's for Clara."

"Clara? Clara's here as well?" He beamed. "Oh, thank god. How is she?"

"She's grand!" Livy said. "We love her to pieces." She poured the tea and set out a plate of Hannah's shortbread.

He thanked her and said, "I'm burning with questions, but they can wait till Kay comes home. She's out with Clara, I suppose?"

"She's volunteering at the Green Lantern."

"The restaurant?"

The question surprised her. As a victim of the explosion, surely he would've known what the Green Lantern had become. "It was a restaurant," she explained, "but it's been turned into a warehouse where people can get new clothes and shoes. Kathleen went to pick out some things for herself and Clara, and when she found out they needed help, she signed up. She goes there every morning, and some afternoons she volunteers at Camp Hill. Hannah looks after Clara."

"Hannah, the housekeeper. Of course. Kay talked a lot about Hannah."

"Sometimes I look after Clara," Livy said. "I love having a little sister, even though she's not mine. Right now they're sledding at the park with Norman."

"Norman? Don't tell me that mutt survived too?" He chuckled again. "Of all the fool names for a dog. I told her, call him Lucky or Buster, not *Norman*." He shook his head. "I never would have believed it. My girls survived. And the boys?" He looked at her hopefully.

Livy shook her head. "I'm sorry…."

Tears filled his eyes and he covered his face with his hands, overcome with emotion.

Livy went into the parlour to give him time to compose himself. She wished the others would come home so Mr. Grant could be with his family.

She sat at the piano and began to play Christmas carols. Quietly, so she wouldn't disturb him. She hadn't touched the piano since the explosion, and Christmas had been the last thing on her mind. Unexpectedly, she found comfort in the familiar carols. As soon as she finished one, she started another. Halfway through "Good King Wenceslas," she was surprised to hear a deep voice behind her, singing:

Page and monarch forth they went
Forth they went together
Through the rude wind's wild lament
And the bitter weather...

At the end of the song, Livy smiled. "Kathleen told me that you used to sing when her mother played the piano. I found one of the keys when I was buried. Your piano was smashed apart."

"You were buried in my house?" He looked puzzled. "What were you doing there at nine in the morning? No disrespect, lass, but we don't often see the likes of you in our neighbourhood. Did Kay forget something?"

He must have read the combination of confusion and unease on her face because he patted her hand and said, "We've a lot to tell, but all in good time. Another carol?"

Livy turned the page to "We Three Kings." As she was playing, she tried to work up the courage to answer his question. It shouldn't be hard to explain why she'd gone to his house. *I've heard a lot about you*, he'd said. Livy hated to think what Kathleen had told him, especially after the vase incident. Knowing that, he'd be pleased to hear that Livy had apologized. But why would he think Kathleen had forgotten something, when she'd lost her job?

There was another question that puzzled her. At the end of the carol, she asked, "Why did you think Kathleen would be here?"

"Because she works here! When I came to after being knocked about, the first thought in my head was, *Thank god Kathleen's safe.* My very thought. I knew the South End wasn't as hard hit because Citadel Hill's in the way. It would've deflected the blast, see? And since Kathleen works here every weekday, I knew she'd be spared."

Livy was stunned. For nearly two weeks Kathleen had let him believe she was still working. Had she been too ashamed to tell him? Thinking that must have been the case, and knowing that *she* was responsible, Livy told him the truth.

"Well then," he said. "I'm right glad I didn't know it at the time. It eased my mind, believing that she was safe." A pause. "I never wanted her to take the job, you see. We had a falling out over it at the time."

He stayed quiet for a moment. Then, "How about 'Silent Night?'"

"Stille Nacht." Dad's favourite. By the end of the first verse Livy's eyes were welling up.

Mr. Grant stopped singing. "What is it?" he said kindly.

She bit her lip and shook her head, unable to speak.

"You must be missing your dad. I heard about the accident. It was a ways back, but I know you're still hurting."

Livy nodded, touched by his understanding. It was the first time anyone had given voice to her loss.

• • •

The Wreck Commission was wearing Will down. How was it possible that so many witnesses had heard, seen, or remembered events so differently? Everyone disagreed on the speed of the ships, their positions, and the exchange of signals. The crew of the *Mont Blanc* disagreed with the survivors of the *Imo*. One witness would say one thing, the next would say the opposite. And what version did the newspapers print? The one that cast the blame on the *Mont Blanc* and her captain and pilot.

No one paid attention to the headlines more than Hannah. For someone who'd ordered him to stop talking about the inquiry, she was quick to bring up the subject whenever the headlines matched her opinion. And that, given the newspapers' slant on things, was all the time.

Tonight Will was determined to beat her to it. The minute he entered the house he called out, "Hannah, I've already seen the headline in the *Herald* and it's a lie. The *Mont Blanc* was *not* exceeding the speed limit. It was the *Imo*."

"Not now, Will!" Hannah's voice came from the parlour.

"And if anyone bothered to read the actual story," he continued, hanging up his coat, "they'd see that the story contradicts its own headline and tells the truth. That's the trouble. People—"

"Will, we've got company!" Livy was coming towards him, smiling broadly. "It's Mr. Grant!"

"What? *Here*?" Will followed his sister into the parlour. There he saw a scarred man in a blue-striped shirt sitting on the sofa, with Clara cuddled up on his lap and Kathleen nestled against his shoulder. Norman lay at his feet.

"Mr. Grant!" Will offered his hand. The instant Mr. Grant smiled, Will recognized him as the playful father he'd seen on Russell Street. Only this time, he was without the gold teeth.

"You must be Will. I want to thank you for taking in my girls, the way you have…all of you." He nodded to Hannah and Livy. "I won't impose myself, but if the girls could stay another night, just until I can make other arrangements…?"

"You're welcome to stay for as long as you like," Will said. "All of you. We've plenty of room. But tell me, how did you manage to survive? I see you've been hurt, but where have you been? Are you able to talk about it?"

"I've told the others, and no harm done, so may as well tell it again." He gave a wry laugh. "Where to begin? I've been here and there and the other place…at the rail yard to start, you know, a regular working day. And after that—

this is what they told me—four days later, some American soldiers who were clearing the wreckage found me wedged between a couple of steel beams and under a turned-over boxcar. I was unconscious but alive, and they took me to the *Old Colony*—the U. S. Army ship they converted to a hospital—and I came to a week later, not there but in St. Mary's. You know, the boys' school. They converted that to a hospital too after the relief train came in, and they moved all the patients from the *Old Colony* there.

"When I came to I couldn't remember a thing. Not my name, age, address, nothing. Something whacked me on the side of my head and I got a concussion. Affected my vision, too. Everything was a blur. Still is a bit. It's only been in the last couple of days that my memory's started to come back."

"That must be why I never saw your name," Kathleen said.

"But you must have read a description of me," said her father. "One of the nurses said she'd put it on the list. You never saw that?"

"I read so many descriptions," Kathleen said. "Men that were dead or unconscious. There weren't many that were as tall as you, with brown hair and blue eyes, and none of them had gold crowns on their two front teeth. I kept looking for the two gold crowns."

He pointed to the gaps where his teeth had been. "They got knocked out, the same as my memory."

"So all this time I should've been looking for a man with two missing front teeth." Kathleen sighed.

"Did you go back, Kay?" he asked after a while. "In case there was anything left?"

"I did," she said. "You need a pass to go into the devastated area, so I got one. There's not a house left standing on Russell Street, or anywhere north of the Barracks. Soldiers all over, in case of looters, and to keep away the gawkers. I found the ruins of our place and did some digging…."

"And…?" He gave her a hopeful look.

"I found a few things, barely enough to fill a shoebox. We're all that's left, Dad. You, me, and Clara."

Clara, now awake, piped up, "*Tingsin shooboss. Noman too.*"

CHAPTER 29

Wednesday, December 19, 1917

By the end of Captain Mackey's third day of testimony, Will had had enough.

Mr. Burchell had hounded Captain Mackey relentlessly. Accused him of being drunk at the time of the collision. Ridiculed him for not being able to spell words in French. Painted him as a coward and a villain for taking to the lifeboat. Yet, in spite of the attacks, the pilot had remained as calm and consistent on the last day as he'd been on the first.

How can he bear it? Will wondered. *Being hounded like that without getting rattled or losing his temper....* He wished he could show as much restraint.

As he was leaving the courthouse, he heard someone shout, "Hey, kid! Got a minute?"

He turned to see a group of junior cadets standing on the corner opposite the courthouse. He didn't recognize the boys, but figured they must be among those volunteering throughout the city.

He crossed over to greet them.

Without so much as a hello, the boy who'd called him over said, "You still going to the trial, sticking up for that murderer?"

The question caught Will off guard. He noticed the burned hands and scarred face of the boy who'd asked, looked around at the others, and decided he'd better tread carefully. All but one had suffered injuries. "Are you volunteering at City Hall?" Will said. "Is that where I've seen you?"

"Don't change the subject," the boy said. "Are you going to the trial?"

"It's an inquiry, not a trial. You know, an investigation—"

"Yeah, we know. Trial, inquiry, same thing."

"They're not the same," Will argued.

"We want to know why you're in favour of Mackey."

The other boys joined in.

"Everyone knows he caused the explosion," said one. "He should be hung from the yardarm, like they used to do with sailors."

"You should be ashamed of yourself, *Wilhelm Schneider.*"

"With a name like that, what do you expect?"

"Look," Will said. "It was an accident. It's not fair to put the blame on one side over the other. If you knew the facts instead of believing the headlines—"

"Here's a fact!" The boy with a broken leg shoved a crutch into Will's chest, almost knocking him over.

"Here's another fact." A boy with his arm in a cast waved it in Will's face.

"Fact is, I'll never hear properly again." A third boy pointed to the bandage covering one ear.

"You know where I've been working?" The boy with no visible injuries spoke for the first time. "I'm at the morgue. The *morgue!* Can you imagine what that's like?"

"Yes!" Will said hotly. "I was in Richmond that day, all right? I saw what happened, same as you. My mum and my sister—" Suddenly, he stopped. It wasn't a competition to see who'd suffered the most, or who had seen the worst of the explosion's aftermath.

"It's a good thing your Mackey is being made to stand trial," the first boy said. "Someone has to take the blame."

The others clamoured their agreement.

"I'm telling you, it's not a trial!" Will protested. "There's no jury. Captain Mackey's not a criminal. It's an inquiry to find out what caused the accident, not who's to blame."

"The *Herald* says—"

"The *Herald* is turning accusations into facts. Look, I can tell you that the reporters are sitting there, same as me, and we're all hearing the same things. Only the reporters make it look like—"

"Why is Mackey still working?" the first boy started again. "Can you answer that? Just the other day, he almost hit another boat. There could have been another explosion."

"Nothing happened!" said Will. "I was down at the harbour and saw it myself. There was no 'narrow escape' like it said in the *Herald*. The ships weren't even close. It's another case of the newspapers twisting the facts."

"It's not right, that Mackey should keep his job."

"Why not? He hasn't been charged. He hasn't been convicted. The war's still on, ships are coming and going, and there's a shortage of pilots. They need him to keep working."

"It still isn't right. But at least he's on trial."

"It's not a *trial!* For the last time—oh, forget it." Will threw up his hands in defeat.

When he got home, he wrote a report for the school newspaper. He explained what had really happened in the "narrow escape" incident and noted that the *Herald* had exaggerated to throw more blame on Captain Mackey.

He read it over, thought about it for a minute, and tossed it out. By the time his school was reopened and the newspaper was back in action, it would be old news. By then, who knew? The newspapers—and public opinion—might have turned against someone else. The war might be over. Pigs might fly.

He flung himself onto his bed feeling depressed and miserable.

"Not now," he said crossly when Livy knocked on his door.

"It's good news, Will," she said. "Mum's coming home tomorrow."

CHAPTER 30

Thursday, December 20, 1917

Livy didn't want to go to Eliza's annual Christmas party. "You've only just come home," she told her mother. "It doesn't feel right to go out and leave you."

"Nonsense," Mum said. "You go and have a good time. And give Eliza's mother my regards." She made an attempt to wink with her good eye. "Find out how the Red Cross is doing without me."

Livy reluctantly agreed. She put on her best dress with the lace trim and let Hannah tie back her hair with a ribbon. After lacing up her boots and putting on her hat and coat, she was ready to go.

"Have you got your torch?" Will said. "It'll be dark by the time you get home."

She pulled it from her pocket and showed him.

"I'm going to town but I'll be back in plenty of time if you want a ride home, or if you want me to walk back with you. Call me from Eliza's if you need me."

"Will! She lives two blocks away, not in Truro!" Livy gave an exasperated sigh.

A short time later she was ringing the bell at Eliza's.

"Livy!" Mrs. Matthews answered the door with a surprised look on her face. "We didn't think you were coming, but how nice to see you. Do come in."

Livy frowned. "Did I get the time wrong? I thought the invitation said three o'clock."

"It did," Mrs. Matthews said, helping her to remove her coat. "It's only that we didn't receive a response from you. Normally, you know...."

Of course, the RSVP.... Livy looked up from removing her boots. She *had* responded to the invitation, saying she'd attend. Hadn't she? "I'm sorry, I thought I'd sent a note."

"Not to worry, dear. It doesn't matter in the slightest, now that you're here. The girls will be delighted to see you. They're in the parlour. You know the way."

After putting on her indoor shoes, Livy smoothed her dress and checked her face in the hall mirror. Some of her hair had come loose, and the curls covered the scar on her forehead. That was a relief. No one would notice and ask how she'd gotten it.

At the entrance to the parlour she paused, taken aback by how festive the room looked. The Christmas tree in the corner, decorated with tinsel, glass balls, and coloured ribbons. The candles, holly, and greeting cards on the mantel. The new glass in the window frames and cedar boughs placed over the top. There was no sign whatsoever that a disaster had struck the city two weeks before.

Eliza and her guests sat around the room, laughing and chatting as they made paper chains from red-, green-, and gold-coloured paper. Livy knew the girls. Rose, Alice, Dorothy, and the others. They were friends from school, church, and the Junior Red Cross. They'd known each other since they were little. They'd made paper chains at Eliza's every Christmas....

Go in, Livy, she told herself. *What are you waiting for?*

I can't. They look too happy.

Stepping into the room would be like stepping back in time. She couldn't do it. She no longer fit in.

Don't be silly. They're your friends.

Her hands felt clammy. She clenched and unclenched her fingers, willing herself to turn around and leave. She was on the verge of doing just that when Eliza looked up and spotted her.

"Livy, at last!" Eliza cried, leaping up and leading Livy by the hand into the room. "Come sit beside me." She patted a place on the sofa. "We're making decorations for the orphanage. Want to help? There's paper and another pair of scissors on the table. We're sharing the glue."

Livy looked at the length of chain coiled in the centre of the room and said, "It looks a mile long already." She *was* late. It was obvious they'd been working on the chain for some time.

She got her supplies and squeezed in between Eliza and Martha. She'd no sooner begun to cut strips of paper than the girls started asking questions.

"How are you, Livy? You never answered my telephone calls."

"Have you been ill? Nobody's seen you for ages."

"I'm fine," she said. "I've been busy." *Doing what?* She hoped they wouldn't ask.

"Have you been to the school?" Rose asked. "The Americans have turned it into a hospital."

"My aunt's volunteering there," said Alice. "I'd like to go see what my classroom looks like with the desks gone. Anyone want to join me?"

"I wouldn't go if you paid me," Martha said. "My cousin was volunteering at Camp Hill but she gave up after two days. Said it was ghastly beyond words."

Eliza's mouth twisted into a look of disgust. "I don't know how anybody could work in a hospital. Or even *be* in one. I get sick just thinking about blood."

Livy cut another strip of paper and looped it into a link of chain, wishing someone would change the subject.

"Not just *blood*. My cousin said she saw a man with his eyeball—"

"Martha, stop!" Beth said. "Livy's here. Her mum lost an eye, remember?"

"I'm sorry, Livy. I wasn't thinking."

"How is your mum?" Eliza asked. "Has it been horrible for her?"

Livy concentrated on cutting another strip. Were her hands shaking, or was she imagining it? "Mum's doing all right. She came home from the hospital this morning. She's got a patch over one eye and in a few months she'll be getting a glass eye."

The girls grimaced.

"It's not so bad," Livy said. "I've seen worse."

There was an awkward silence. Livy met the quizzical looks on the girls' faces but remained silent. She hadn't told anyone the full story of what she had experienced that day, and she wasn't about to start now. Not here, not in this company.

She set down the scissors and folded her hands in her lap. They were definitely shaking. Had anyone noticed?

Suddenly Eliza jumped up and clapped her hands. "Let's play Forfeits! Livy's right. This chain is plenty long enough." With the others' help, she cleared the room to make space.

Forfeits was a favourite game, and one they had played countless times before. Eliza produced a hat filled with penalties written on pieces of paper, and Beth was chosen to be the judge. She went into the hall while the others each put a small personal item on the carpet.

When Beth returned, she chose an item and held it up. "Here I have a priceless white handkerchief trimmed with the finest lace. What must the owner do to redeem it?"

"It's mine!" Martha said. She reached into the hat and read out her penalty. "*Crawl under the table and bark like a dog, quack like a duck, and snort like a pig*. Not all at the same time, I hope!"

The penalty was paid, with plenty of giggles, and Beth moved on to another item. Over the next several minutes, Alice had to repeat "Great glass globes gleam green" ten times, Alice had to touch her nose with her tongue to get back her hair ribbon, and Eliza had to sing "Jingle Bells" while meowing like a cat.

Even Livy was laughing by the time Beth held up the final item. "Now I come to this beee-utiful silver chain with a silver heart, engraved with the letter O."

"That's mine," Livy said, and reached out a hand to claim it.

"Not so fast!" Beth laughed. "What must the owner do to redeem it?" She reached into the hat and drew out of slip of paper: "*Sing a Christmas carol in a foreign language*."

"Not an animal language, like barking," said Eliza. "We've had that already and my stomach hurts from laughing so hard."

Livy thought for a moment. She wished her penalty had been something nonsensical that would make everyone laugh, but she had to play by the rules. She knew a couple of French carols from school, but there was only one carol she liked to sing in a foreign language, and that was "Silent Night" in German.

"Come on, Livy," Eliza said. "We're waiting."

Livy stood up. Everyone was staring and, to avoid making eye contact, she fixed her gaze on the star shining on top of the Christmas tree. *This is for you, Dad*, she said silently, and began to sing the words he'd taught her. "*Stille Nacht! Heil'ge Nacht! Alles schläft....*"

Livy heard a rustling and some intakes of breath. She carried on, thinking that the girls were admiring both her singing and her language ability. She'd only gotten through one verse when Mrs. Matthews burst into the room, yelling, "Olivia Schneider! Stop this at once!" Her face was livid. "What in the name of heaven are you thinking?"

Livy felt as though she'd been kicked in the stomach. "My dad...." Her voice trembled. "It's only a language."

"It's *German*!" Mrs. Matthews snapped. "It would have had your father arrested if he were still alive. You know what we think of the Germans! Not another word of that filthy language, do you hear?"

"Oh, Livy," Eliza said crossly after her mother had gone. "You should have known better. You could have sung something in French."

For a long time no one spoke. Some of the girls looked away. Others examined their fingernails.

I should leave, Livy thought. From the moment she'd arrived, she'd felt as if she were outside herself, watching a stranger play the part of a Livy she no longer knew.

"One more game and then we'll have supper," said Eliza. "Any requests?"

"Do you mean for games or for supper?" Martha asked.

Everyone laughed, and the mood lightened.

"Let's play Blind Man's Bluff," Martha continued. "I'll go first."

Eliza put the blindfold over Martha's eyes, spun her around three times, and, after telling her not to knock over the Christmas tree, set her loose.

Livy had always loved the game but, this time, she wanted no part in it. She skirted aside whenever "it" got too close, even if that meant bumping another girl out of her way. For several rounds she was successful. But finally, she was caught.

She moved into the centre and Martha put on the blindfold. "Remember Dominion Day, Livy? When we were playing this at the church party, and you tagged Lewis?"

"He was so happy!" someone else said. "That must've been when he started to follow you."

Livy turned her head, wanting to know who was speaking.

"Stand still!" Martha scolded. "I'm trying to tie the blindfold and you keep squirming."

"He had such a crush on you. My mum said he was 'smitten.' We used to see him go past our house, trying to catch up to you."

Amy. She lived on the same street as Lewis, a block away from Livy's.

"You'd get so mad!" Amy continued. "Remember, Livy? How you'd yell at him to leave you alone? You'd call him the worst names, and laugh at him, but he never cared."

"There!" Martha said. "Does that feel all right?"

Livy nodded, although the blindfold was too tight. Uncomfortably so, but she couldn't bring herself to speak. Her mouth was dry. Her throat was tight. Her stomach ached.

"I'm going to spin you around now," Martha said. "Ready? One…two…three—"

Not yet, I'm not ready!

"Go!"

Dizzy, confused by the darkness, Livy felt herself being pushed towards one side of the room. She took a step to regain her balance. She could sense that the girls were moving around to confuse her, their footsteps soft on the carpet, their hands clapping close to her ears, their voices disorienting her with sighs and whispers.

"Remember Lewis," someone teased in a singsong voice. "He thought you liked him. He told everybody that you could see through the blindfold and picked him on purpose."

Livy whirled around, her arms stretched out to tag the speaker. Her fingers brushed against a branch of the Christmas tree. Panicking, she spun around too quickly in the opposite direction. The sudden movement made her head swim. She flung out an arm to steady herself. The girls were laughing, getting louder, moving faster. She swung her arm again, this time striking a large and heavy object that hit the floor with a resonating crash.

Suddenly she was on the ground in the dark, screaming that she couldn't move, that the house had fallen on top of her and she was trapped, smelling smoke, knowing that she wasn't alone. "Keep looking!" she kept screaming. "Peter's down here! Don't leave him behind!"

"Mum, come quick! It's Livy! Call a doctor!"

Livy tore off the blindfold. Someone was holding her, telling her to stop crying, telling her that everything was fine, but it wasn't, *she* wasn't, she couldn't stop crying, she'd never be able to stop.

• • •

After seeing Livy off, Will had walked to town to buy a few Christmas gifts. With everyone in the house suffering a loss, it would be a simple, quiet Christmas. It was impossible for it to be otherwise. No one was in the mood to be merry. But a small gift for everyone wouldn't go amiss and, for Clara's sake, they had to have a tree and maybe hang up stockings.

Having Mr. Grant at the house had done wonders to cheer Kathleen, Will thought, as well as Hannah, Livy, and himself. As for his mother…he chuckled, amazed at how well she'd taken to having the Grants in the house, and how much she seemed to enjoy Mr. Grant's company. So far, at least. It was still early days.

He was mulling over Christmas and what more they could do when he saw Henry coming out of the druggist's. "How are you?" he asked. It had been a week since they'd seen each other. Will told Henry about his mum being home from Bellevue Hospital and Mr. Grant having shown up out of the blue.

"Speaking of the Bellevue," Henry said. "You hear about the survivor from the *Imo*? It's all over the newspapers."

"No more papers for me," Will said. "It's nothing but rumours and lies."

"Not this time. It's the helmsman of the *Imo*. Johnson, Johansen, something like that. He was in Bellevue Hospital. That's why I thought you might have heard. They arrested him for murder, and now he's in jail."

"What?" Will gaped. "Who did he murder?"

"They say he murdered the *Imo*'s captain and Pilot Hayes, then steered the ship straight at the *Mont Blanc*."

Will scoffed. "What proof do they have?"

"They found a German book in his possession."

"For gosh sake, Henry! Johansen's not a German name. It's Norwegian. The *Imo*'s a Norwegian ship. And since when are the police in Halifax experts on reading German? Don't you think it's possible the book was in Norwegian?"

"I'm just saying what I heard," Henry said. "Makes sense to me."

Will decided not to press the issue. "How's Lewis?"

"He's making progress. Still in Camp Hill but he should be home sometime in the New Year, crutches and all."

"He was some lucky," Will said. "There's no accounting for it, is there? The way some survived."

"Lewis asked about Livy, by the way. He saw her heading off to Richmond that morning. He was certain she'd been killed."

"She's doing all right. Today's the first time since the explosion she's gone out to see her friends. I'll tell her that Lewis was asking about her."

"That'll cheer *him* up, but I don't know about Livy." Henry grinned. "Tell her she's safe for a while. He won't be catching up to her on crutches."

Will laughed. "I wouldn't rule it out."

He thought about Livy on the way home, and hoped she was enjoying herself at the party. It wasn't like her to avoid her friends, the way she'd been doing. He hoped today would be a turning point.

CHAPTER 31

December 24–27, 1917

Four days had passed since Livy had been brought home from Eliza's party, examined by the doctor, and told she had to have plenty of bed rest. The doctor had found nothing physically wrong with her but, after learning of her experience in Richmond, he determined that she was suffering from shell shock. Like half the population in the city, he'd told them, not to mention the soldiers returning from the front. Darkness could trigger an attack. And loud, sudden noises.

After four days in bed, sleeping and eating nothing but soup and rice pudding, Livy had had enough. She got up, dressed, and went downstairs, stopping when she overheard Hannah in the parlour.

"I knew it, Fiona, I knew it." Hannah sniffed loudly. "I told Livy she was overdoing it, right from the start I told her, carrying on like everything was normal. You can only be brave for so long, I told her. You can keep saying you're fine, you're fine, but sooner or later it'll catch up with you, I told her…." Another loud sniff.

"Will told her the same—a real prince, he's been, bless his heart—but no, Livy wouldn't listen. And of course Will didn't want to worry you about it, not with your suffering and your poor eye…I'm sorry. And now this!" She broke down into another round of sobs.

"Dear Hannah," Mum said. "You did your best. We'd be lost without you. Go have yourself a cup of tea. I'll go upstairs and sit with Livy until she wakes up."

"No need, Mum," Livy said, walking in on them. She smiled. "Don't look so shocked. I feel better. Honest! You've said so yourself, Hannah. There's nothing better than having a good cry."

"I never meant for two whole entire days!" Hannah said. "Or having the shakes at the same time!"

"They stopped after two days. Then I slept for a full day and was bored the day after that. Now I feel fine. See?" She held out her arms. "No shaking."

"We'll see," Hannah grumbled. "First sign of a tremor, I'm marching you back to bed." She left the room, still grumbling.

"She's right, you know," Mum said. "We've been worried about you."

'I know," said Livy, joining her mother on the sofa. "How are you, Mum?"

"Every day is better than the one before. See how the swelling's going down? It's hard to keep from bumping into things though. While you were in bed—funny, but I rather enjoyed being the visitor instead of the patient for a change. What was I saying?"

"While I was in bed...."

"Oh, yes. The others made some paths for me to follow, to help me get from one room to another, and they're making sure that Clara's toys are never in the way. Mr. Grant told me he almost broke his neck when he first arrived." She smiled.

"I can walk around with you a bit, if you like," Livy offered.

"Actually...I'd like to sit here and think, while you play the piano."

"Really?" Livy's face lit up.

"Some Christmas carols would be lovely."

Livy played one carol after another while her mother hummed along or listened in silence. She couldn't keep her body from tensing up whenever she hit a wrong note, but the expected rebuke never came.

"I never gave you enough credit," Mum said after a while. "You practiced so hard and you play so well...but I never told you."

"Mum...."

"Your father did," she continued. "I guess that's why you kept on. He was good at giving praise and encouragement. Wasn't he? My father wasn't, neither was my mother. That's why I can't play the piano. I gave up. I admire you for keeping on."

Livy was astounded. Her mother was a new person. Was it because she had the time to be still and to think about all that had happened? She got up from the piano and gave her mum a hug. Not too tight. But tight enough.

Livy was still playing carols when Mr. Grant came in with a fir tree. He'd bought it at Mum's insistence. It wouldn't be Christmas as usual, but they had to have a tree for Clara. Even Hannah agreed, and promised she wouldn't gripe about the needles she'd have to sweep from the carpet.

They waited until after Clara was asleep before decorating the tree, so that she'd get up the next morning for Christmas and see it transformed with strings of lights, silver stars, ornaments of coloured glass, and a golden angel at the top.

• • •

On Christmas Day they had a roast turkey with all the trimmings and Hannah's plum pudding. It didn't seem that long ago that Livy had been helping Hannah make the pudding. Stir-up Sunday, she remembered, the day after Lewis had followed her to Point Pleasant Park. She'd dropped in the traditional silver coin that would bring luck to the person who found it, and she and Will had joined Hannah in stirring the pudding mixture. Just the three of them, as Mum had gone to a meeting at the church. They'd talked about Dad and how much he'd loved the ritual, stirring from east to west in honour of the three kings who had travelled from the east. He used to snatch the odd raisin from the bowl when Hannah wasn't looking, and when she caught him (more often than not), she'd rap his knuckles playfully with the wooden spoon. *Christmas won't be the same without your dad*, she'd said that day.

Livy looked at those gathered round the table and marvelled. Never, in a hundred million years, could she have imagined how not-the-same this Christmas would turn out to be.

• • •

Lewis was asleep when Livy arrived at Camp Hill Hospital a few days later. His head was still bandaged and one leg was encased in plaster. A crooked line of stitches scrawled down one arm. He looked smaller than she remembered.

She was standing at his bedside, wondering whether she should stay or come back later, when he opened his eyes. He looked confused, as if trying to remember who she was. Then his face split into the grin she had once found so irritating.

She choked back a sob. "I'm sorry, Lewis."

"What for?"

For being mean to you, for making fun of you, for telling you to get lost.... She couldn't bring herself to say it out loud. "Do you feel all right? I can leave if you want to go back to sleep."

"No, don't go."

For a few moments they didn't speak. Then Lewis asked if it was cold outside. Yes, it was. Livy asked if the hospital food was okay. Yes, it was. No, actually, it was terrible.

They shared a laugh and another long silence.

At the same moment, both spoke at once.

"When you were going to Richmond—"

"When you went down to the harbour—"

"You first," Livy said.

He told her how the blast had thrown him into a pile of lumber on the dock with his leg twisted underneath. "So I'm lying there, wondering, how am I going to get out of this? That's when the wave comes...sweeps me up...and I'm thinking, this is the end for me. Next thing I know, the wave's thrown me back to shore but in a different place. And after a while I was found. Battered up pretty bad." He shrugged. "That's about it. I don't really like to talk about it."

"Me neither," said Livy, but found herself telling him about her experience, the way she'd told Kathleen. "I told my family I was buried. That's all. I never talk about how I felt or what I saw after I was rescued. Maybe one day."

"Me too," Lewis said. "But not today."

They talked about other things. School, church, and friends. Activities they used to enjoy doing, and might again. Going to Point Pleasant Park, taking the ferry across the Narrows to Dartmouth. She told him about Eliza's party and how out of place she'd felt.

He nodded. "I feel the same, even with my family."

"I'm glad you're okay," Livy said as she was leaving. "I hope you can go home soon."

She was walking to town when she noticed several people ahead of her on the sidewalk stop without warning and change direction. Some crossed to the other side of the street. Others went back the way they had come.

She saw a short, stocky man with a mustache coming towards her. She knew at once who he was. Will had pointed him out to her often enough, long before the explosion had ever happened.

Without a second thought she said, "Hello, Captain Mackey."

He nodded and gave her a friendly smile as he walked past.

CHAPTER 32

Late January 1918

After a long holiday break, the Wreck Commission resumed its inquiry. Will decided not to attend. He'd go back to the courthouse for the closing arguments, but not before.

He and Livy spent time with their mum, helping her get around both inside and outside the house. The vision in her left eye was gradually improving, but she still needed help avoiding people and objects, and going up or down the stairs. Without peripheral vision, crossing the street was hazardous. She complained of being clumsy and having no hand-eye coordination. Still, she persevered, determined to carry on as she had before. Anyone who suggested she might *not* be able to do so was told emphatically that she'd lost an eye, not her mind. "As long as I can move and think, I'll do what needs doing. And that's final."

She would not hear of Joe Grant moving out, and was pleased when he decided not to accept his sister's invitation to move his family to Vancouver. With Will's assistance, he was tackling numerous repair jobs around the house, many of which had been left undone since her husband had gone. What with all the rebuilding, reconstructing, and repairing going on throughout the city—and the building of temporary apartments for the homeless—labourers and skilled workers were impossible to find. Joe Grant was a godsend. He didn't know when he'd be able to return to his job at the rail yards. He tired easily and could only work for an hour or two at a stretch. Working alongside him, Will noticed that he blacked out sometimes, though he continued to function. Afterwards, he would not remember what he'd been doing or how much time had passed. He admitted to having severe headaches, but seldom complained.

The schools had yet to be reopened. Livy's was still being used as a hospital and Will's school on Morris Street was full of injured patients. He often wondered if he should forget about going back to school and get a job. His mother told him not to be a daft fool.

One day in town, Will crossed paths with Edward Beazley. He knew that Edward would be giving testimony at the inquiry and wished him well.

"You're a day too late," Edward said glumly. "I got a good grilling yesterday. That Mr. Burchell—well, you've had a taste of him, haven't you?"

Will hadn't noticed Edward in the courthouse, and hated to think that he'd witnessed Will's humiliating ordeal. "After he grilled the examining officer," Edward continued, "I got it good. I didn't mind hearing Mr. Wyatt get pulled apart, but when that Burchell gave *me* a scolding, right there in public—"

"Was that because you stopped reporting on the outgoing ships?" Will recalled how proud Edward had been when he'd told him about his decision.

Edward nodded. "My 'fancied grievances,' as Burchell put it. As if I'd *imagined* the clerks laughing at me. And of course he made fun of my age, same as he did with you."

Will didn't want to be reminded. "How do you think it'll turn out?"

"Is there any doubt? It's a kangaroo court. The judge made up his mind weeks ago. They want a scapegoat and it's going to be Captain Mackey."

• • •

At the end of January, Will attended the inquiry to hear the closing arguments. He expected that Mr. Burchell would paint the pilot and the captain of the *Mont Blanc* in a bad light, but had no idea how vicious he would be.

He called Captain Le Medec "a crazy Frenchman." He accused Captain Mackey of perjury. He blamed the "stupid crazy collision" entirely on the *Mont Blanc* for being in the *Imo*'s waters.

Judge Drysdale's decision was what everyone had expected. Pilot Mackey and Captain Le Medec were responsible for violating the rules of the road. Their negligence caused the collision. The collision caused the explosion.

Moments after the judge delivered his decision, the two men were arrested and charged with manslaughter and criminal negligence. So was Chief Examining Officer Wyatt.

"It's about time," spectators were saying as they filed out of the courtroom. "They got what they deserved."

• • •

"That's the end of it for now," Will told his family, after describing the events of the day. "Captain Mackey's in jail. The other two men paid the bail and got out, but Mr. Mackey didn't have enough money. That's what I heard. He gave up his pilot's license. I don't know what happens next."

"He should rot in jail," Hannah muttered. "Hanging's too good for him."

Her comments were ignored.

"The judge must have said the *Imo* was partly to blame," Livy said.

"Nope. He never said a word about the *Imo* being on the wrong side of the harbour. He said the entire crew of the *Imo* was blameless because they were killed. Said he couldn't blame Pilot Hayes for anything because he's not here to defend himself."

"So if everybody on the *Mont Blanc* had been killed, then nobody would be blamed?"

Will scoffed. "They would have picked on somebody else, like Mr. Wyatt. He would've been the scapegoat."

"I guess that's what Captain Mackey did wrong," Livy said. "He survived."

CHAPTER 33

February 1918

Early in February, Livy's mum had decided it was time to start volunteering again. "Only for the Halifax Relief Commission," she told her family. "Light tasks only, so don't worry. A bit of paperwork, a few visits to the North End with another volunteer. No more working with a hundred other societies. And I will continue with the Red Cross—that 'hotbed of suffragettes' as your father put it, bless him."

Livy was disappointed, even though her mum was still home a good portion of the time. She enjoyed having her mother there, especially since the schools still hadn't reopened.

They spent long hours talking to each other and, during one such conversation, Livy learned what had happened to her mother that terrible day. She'd been visiting a single mother in her Richmond apartment and had joined the children at the window to watch the fire. It was all she remembered until she'd woken up on a stretcher unable to see. More than that, she couldn't or wouldn't say. She was still trying to learn the fate of the children and their mother.

Livy often read out loud to her, since reading for prolonged periods was a strain.

Other times, Mum told her stories about Livy's dad, when he was a new arrival from Germany, and Hannah, when she'd arrived as a young girl to work for Livy's grandparents.

The relationship they had was almost too good to be true. Livy knew it could change, and likely would change, in one way or another. But she was certain that it would not go back to the way it had been before.

One morning, as Mum was getting ready to go out, she said, "I made a resolution while I was in the hospital. Once I got over that dreadful period of confusion, and the terrifying news that I was going to lose my sight—thankfully, that didn't happen—I came to my senses. I accepted that I'd lost one eye and I started to reflect. I realized that I haven't been a particularly nice person, especially not to you—"

"*Mum!* Don't say that…."

"Hear me out. We know it's true. I was narrow-minded, critical, and impatient. I had two good eyes but I never saw beyond my side of a story. Now I'm going to make the reverse of that true. I'll try to see two sides of a story with my one good eye. What do you think?"

Livy was speechless.

"Smile, Livy. It was supposed to make you happy. Now I'm off to work." She adjusted the patch that covered her empty eye socket, picked up her cane, and kissed Livy goodbye.

Livy watched from the window, pleased at how well her mum was adapting. She was steady on her feet, no longer bumping into things, and her spirits were good.

Since she'd started to work for the Relief Commission, she'd managed to locate many of the people she'd assisted in the North End, and made sure they knew about the relief that was available. She helped them, and others, make claims for housing, furniture, clothing, and pensions.

One such person was Mr. Grant. With Mum's help, he'd applied for one of the new temporary apartments being built on the Exhibition Grounds. The speed with which workers were putting up the apartments astounded everyone. Especially since they were doing it in winter. Even more astounding were the temporary apartments built on the Commons, where soldiers had dug shovels into the frozen ground a mere three days after the explosion. Those apartments had been finished within a month.

A few days earlier, Mr. Grant had found out that his application had been approved. He, Kathleen, and Clara would be moving in March.

• • •

"Are you still coming, Livy?" Kathleen ran down the stairs, dressed to go outside.

"Won't take a minute," Livy said.

They were soon on their way to the Massachusetts-Halifax Relief warehouse. The night before, the two families had celebrated the news of the Grants' apartment and Livy was happy to accompany Kathleen to the warehouse to pick out furniture.

Kathleen could not hold back her excitement. "Dad says I can get whatever I want, but I'm not to overdo it because we've only got five rooms and they're small. It'll be grand to look and see what's there. All of it's brand new, all of it's free, and we can keep it forever. Most of it's come all the way from Massachusetts."

"I'll be sorry to see you go," said Livy. "You and your dad and Clara."

"What?" Kathleen's eyes widened. "Hasn't your mum told you? She's hiring me as her assistant to help with the paperwork. It's a strain on her eye, as you know, so I'll be writing letters, filling out claims forms—there's some people who can't read or write, especially some of the widows, and most of that I'll be doing right in your own house."

"You'll be a personal secretary?"

Kathleen laughed. "That sounds much too posh, but let's call it that anyway. I'll be doing some of the housework as well, and she'll be paying me double what I earned before because—here's the best part—she thinks I should finish my education and do better for myself. Maybe even go to college one day. What do you think about that?"

For the second time that day, Livy was speechless.

"You know the other best part?" Kathleen continued. "She says I can bring Clara when I come to work here. She's talked it over with Hannah and Hannah is thrilled to pieces."

"What about Norman? Mum can't have agreed to that."

"Livy, where have you been that you haven't heard any of this? We're not allowed pets in the apartment so Norman is staying with you."

Three times speechless. Livy threw her arms around Kathleen, hoping she wouldn't burst into tears.

When they entered the warehouse, their jaws dropped. It was a treasure trove. Bedroom suites with iron or brass bedsteads, solid oak bureaux with mirrors, and washstands to match. Dining tables, high chairs, and chairs with carved backs. Parlour tables, sofas and armchairs, desks, kitchen cupboards, and every possible dish or piece of cutlery you'd need to fill those cupboards.

In another part of the warehouse there were curtains, cushions, window shades, lamps, carpets, and everything else one might need to furnish a home. Kathleen gasped. "Where do I start?"

"I'll spin you around," said Livy. "Wherever you're facing when I stop, that's where you start."

It wasn't long before Kathleen was putting her name and apartment number on pieces of furniture so that they could be delivered.

Livy left her to it. She was strolling through the warehouse, wondering what she'd choose if she had to, when she heard someone say, "Hello, South End girl."

She looked up and saw a girl's reflection in a mirror, close to where she was standing. The red hair and impish grin were unmistakable. "You're Jane," she said. "At least I think that's right."

"It is! And you're Olivia, but everyone calls you Livy."

"You called me Liv." She smiled. "I like your coat." It was wool, similar to the one Livy had been wearing that day, right down to the pearl buttons. The blue colour matched Jane's eyes and looked grand against her hair. "It suits you."

"Thanks," Jane beamed and did a twirl. "I got it at the Green Lantern. It came all the way from Boston—brand new! Soon as I saw it, I said, that's the one for me."

"I think I saw you at Camp Hill Hospital." Livy immediately wished she hadn't brought that up, as it wasn't a place Jane would likely want to remember. Jane looked better than she had then, although the lower part of her face showed burn scars.

She saw where Livy was looking. "I know. I'm a right holy fright. Still better than some. And better than I was. That time at Camp Hill? I thought it might be you. I was right stunned to see you walking about. I thought you were going to Russell Street that day."

"I was. I got there." She changed the subject. "The boys who were with you?"

"All gone."

"I'm sorry." Acting on impulse, Livy said, "Would you like to come to my house for tea?"

"Yes, please! If you're not too far. My leg's still a bother."

Livy walked slowly to match Jane's pace, noticing that she had a limp.

As they made their way to the South End, Jane talked about her family. Parents, brothers and sisters, aunts and uncles, and cousins. The ones she'd lost in the explosion, the ones who'd survived, and the ones who were fighting in France and had missed it. Unless they'd been killed over there and she hadn't yet heard. When she finished, she said, "I know something about you."

Livy looked surprised.

"Your mum is Mrs. Schneider. I saw you downtown the other day. She lost an eye. She's the one helped us get one of the apartments on the Commons. We've never lived anywhere new before. My mum, two brothers, and me. We're all that's left out of ten. Our building fell down in the explosion so we had to live at my Auntie Nell's and it was some cramped, let me tell you. Your mum found us there. The witch, we called her. She used to be a right holy terror."

Livy bristled. Who did Jane think she was, talking about Livy's mum that way? Especially after being invited for tea?

"We hated it when she came around," Jane continued. "She'd look inside our cupboards for drink. Once she found some of Pa's whiskey—he only had it for a toothache—but that was it, no help for us that month." She shrugged. "That's the way it was. Still is, you know. They say the relief they're giving out is fair to everyone, but it's not."

Livy had never heard anyone her age speak so frankly. As for calling her mother a witch....

She was thinking of an excuse to call off the invitation when Jane said, "I'm only telling you this because your mum's different now. We were ready to shut the door in her face when she came 'round to Auntie Nell's, but your mum said she was sorry for this and for that and for a lot of other things, and she put us at the top of the list for housing. The very top! Said she knows that families like ours are sometimes at the bottom even though they shouldn't be. That's how we got our new apartment. I wanted to tell you. We don't call her the witch anymore."

For the fourth time in as many hours, Livy was speechless.

Jane was already on a new topic. "I have to go to the South End for school next month. Mine was demolished and a lot of us kids are being sent to Tower Road School." She grimaced. "Can you picture me in the South End? I'm some nervous. Is Tower Road where you go?"

"No, but my brother Will's going there. His school's full of injured patients. I go to the Halifax Ladies' College."

"Oh, my," Jane teased, turning up her nose. "Lawdy-dawdy."

Livy laughed. "It's not as grand as that." (Though it was.)

No one was home when they reached her house, so Livy played hostess and served tea and cake in the parlour. "I never would have done this before—"

She stopped and lowered her cup, her hand trembling. *Not again, not now....*

"Before the explosion?" Jane said. Her face was grave. "It's always there, isn't it?"

Livy nodded. Before she knew it, she was telling Jane everything about that day and the ones that followed. The nightmares, the panic, the unshakeable feeling that Kathleen's brother had been with her in the ruins but left behind.

The girls were still talking when Will came home. After being introduced to Jane and told that they would be at the same school, he offered her a ride home.

"You've a motorcar?" Jane's face lit up. "I've never been in one! Wait till I tell my brothers!"

Livy watched them drive off. She felt better after talking to Jane, the way she had with Lewis and Kathleen—three people with whom she'd shared more than the "buried and rescued" version of her experience. Before the unthinkable happened, she never would have spoken to them beyond a "hello" to Kathleen or a "get lost" to Lewis. She might have met Jane on her way to Russell Street, but spending time with her, like today? That never would have happened.

She thought about Jane and Kathleen and all they'd lost. Before the explosion, Kathleen had lost her mother. Livy had lost her father.

He's not coming back, Livy realized. *He won't appear at our doorway. He's missing, lost at sea, gone. There won't be a happy ending.*

She had to accept it, the way thousands of others were accepting their loss.

She thought about all the different circumstances that had led up to the explosion. If they'd been different, if even *one* circumstance had changed....

If the *Mont Blanc* hadn't been caught in a storm and delayed on her way from New York, she wouldn't have had to spend the night outside the submarine nets.

If the coaling ship that had fuelled up the *Imo* hadn't been delayed, the *Imo* would have been able to leave the day before.

If the *Imo* hadn't been on the wrong side of the harbour, if one or the other ship had moved out of the way, the collision wouldn't have happened.

If the collision hadn't happened, there would not have been a fire.

If there hadn't been a fire, the ship would not have blown up.

Every little thing led to something else. A chain of circumstances building into a disaster.

Livy followed the chain backwards to what she saw as the starting point. It wasn't the fault of Captain Mackey or the *Imo* or the dockworkers in New York who had loaded the explosives onto the *Mont Blanc.* The start of it was the man in Europe who fired the shot that killed an archduke and made the Kaiser of Germany start the war. A war that needed explosives.

Closer to home, there was another chain of circumstances—the one that had started with a broken vase and taken her to the North End.

A car door slammed. Seeing that Will had returned, she ran out to greet him, eager to hear what he had to say about Jane. She was glad that Jane would know someone from the South End at her new school, especially since she was feeling nervous. Livy wished it could be her instead of her brother.

CHAPTER 34

March 1918

"He's free to go!" Will announced. "The Supreme Court of Nova Scotia has made its decision." He sat down with the *Herald* to read the details.

He'd been awaiting the outcome of the court case with some trepidation, given what had happened during the inquiry, but he needn't have worried. Judge Russell (not Drysdale, thank goodness) had straight away dismissed the testimony of the Wreck Commission, saying it had been an inquiry, not a trial. He heard from seven new witnesses and found that there was no criminal evidence against CEO Wyatt, Captain Le Medec, or Captain Mackey. He said that Captain Mackey hadn't been negligent or careless.

He'd done everything possible to prevent the collision. Best of all, Judge Russell ruled that the collision was caused by the conduct of the *Imo*. The three men were free to go.

Will was delighted. At the same time, he knew the decision would be unpopular.

"Are you going to town today?"

"Huh?" Will looked up from the paper to see Livy standing over him, hands on her hips.

"I've asked you three times already. Aren't you going to get your school supplies?"

"Sorry, Livy. I was reading about the trial. The judge said—"

"Tell me later. I need things too and want to know when you're leaving so I can walk with you."

"Oh, heck. I forgot all about school supplies. I'm leaving now."

As they were walking, Will thought about going back to school. He was sorry his own school wasn't ready to re-open but, at the same time, he was looking forward to going to Tower Road School. It would be interesting, what with students from the North End attending. Tough for them, though. Losing everything, then having to go to a school in the South End....

A thought crossed his mind.

"Livy, I want your opinion. I'm thinking of starting a school newspaper at Tower Road. I'll interview the kids who've come from the North End and ask them—"

"No!" she argued. "It'll be too hard for them."

"They don't have to say anything if they don't want to, but I could tell them I was there."

"Interview yourself, then." Seeing his crestfallen expression, she added, "Sorry. I just think it's too soon. You should ask Jane what she thinks." She chuckled. "I guarantee she'll give you her honest opinion. I like her. Don't you? She's a change from my other friends."

She told Will how they'd met, surprised she hadn't told him before. In return, she had to listen to him talk about the trial.

They parted ways when they got to town, Livy to the department store to buy a new school uniform, and Will to the stationer's to buy scribblers and a bottle of ink.

He was waiting at the cash register when he spotted Captain Mackey on the other side of the street. Two men were charging towards the pilot, leaving him no alternative but to jump out of the way. One man spat, the other shouted rude comments. Other pedestrians were crossing the street to avoid the pilot or staring at him with openly hostile looks. He never once lowered his head or altered his pace.

Will hurriedly paid for his purchases and ran out to catch up with the pilot. "How are you, Captain Mackey? I just wanted to say I'm glad you've been released, and that the judge said it wasn't your fault. I never thought it was."

"Thanks, Will. I appreciate that."

"Murderer!" a voice shouted from across the street.

Captain Mackey paid no attention.

"Are you piloting again?" Will asked.

"No, I'm sorry to say. They haven't given me back my license. So I'm doing whatever jobs I can find. By the way, Will, I was at the marina the other day and saw your dad's sailboat. You've painted on a new name."

"*Seabird,*" Will said. "A translation from the original name. We thought it would be easier."

The captain nodded. "I see your point. No use drawing attention when there's no need. She's a fine-looking sailboat. You'll be taking her out soon, I expect?"

"Soon as the weather warms up. We're planning a bit of a ceremony, Mum, Livy, Hannah, and me, as a way of saying goodbye to my dad. It's hard, not being able to have a proper burial."

"Right hard indeed, Will. You have my condolences. He was a good man, your dad."

They talked about their respective families until they reached the store where Will was to meet Livy. "Good luck, Captain Mackey," he said. "Getting your license back and all. They've no reason to keep it from you now."

• • •

Livy was playing the piano later that afternoon when Kathleen entered the parlour.

"Sorry to interrupt," she said, "but I've just finished packing and want to show you something before I leave.

Remember the day I went to the devastated area? I'd heard of things being found in the ruins. Letters and photographs that were still intact, pieces of china without so much as a chip. I didn't expect to find anything, not after the fire, but look."

She unwrapped a small vase. "It's only cut glass, not fine crystal like the one you had. But of all our possessions, this is the one that reminds me most of my mother. I gave it to her for her birthday a few years back. She loved it. She had it on the windowsill in the kitchen, always with a sprig of flowers or a small branch with berries. It would catch the evening sun when she was getting supper ready. A happy vase, she used to say."

"It's beautiful," Livy said. "It catches the light every bit as well as the vase I broke."

"Well...here. I'd like you to have it. To thank you for being with Clara and...well, everything."

Livy struggled to hold back her tears. "I can't. It's all you have to remember your mum."

"Truly, I want you to have it. Your house gets more sunlight than our apartment does. And I'll be coming here most days, so I'll see it." She reached into her pocket and drew out the piano key. "Besides, I've got this. Mum played beautifully. Like you do."

Livy nodded her thanks and set the vase on the desk. *An inexpensive vase. A piano key. A knitted scarf. The smallest things that remind us....*

"How did I survive?"

She hadn't realized she'd spoken out loud until Kathleen said, "I don't know. But you did. Now you have to make it matter."

"I will," said Livy. "I promise." The morning sun struck the glass vase and made it sparkle. A rainbow shimmered across her hands.

AUTHOR'S NOTE

At 9:04:35 on the morning of December 6, 1917, Halifax, Nova Scotia, fell victim to the world's single largest man-made explosion—the largest, that is, until the atomic bomb was dropped on Hiroshima in 1945. What were the circumstances that caused the ravages of the Great War (1914–1918) to strike at the heart of this North American city?

At the time, Halifax was one of the busiest and most prosperous ports in the British Empire. Ships of all description passed through its harbour, transporting troops, horses, supplies, and munitions overseas. By late 1917, the situation in Europe was desperate. The demand for munitions was so great that even battered old ships were pressed into service. One such ship was a French steamer called *Mont Blanc.*

After picking up munitions in New York, the *Mont Blanc* was meant to travel with a convoy across the Atlantic. The ship was deemed to be too slow, however, and its captain, Aimé Le Medec, was ordered to join a convoy in Halifax.

Late in the afternoon on December 5, the *Mont Blanc*, having been delayed by a storm, reached the mouth of Halifax Harbour. Local pilot Francis Mackey boarded the ship and directed her to a nearby examination boat. An examining officer inspected the ship's manifest, which listed a lethal assortment of explosives: 2,300 tons of wet and dry picric acid, 200 tons of TNT, ten tons of gun cotton, and 35 tons of benzol (a high-octane gasoline), as well as 300 live rounds of ammunition. As it was not unusual for ships to be carrying munitions and explosives in and out of Halifax Harbour during wartime, the *Mont Blanc* passed the inspection. She was forced to anchor outside the safety of the harbour, however, as the anti-submarine gates had closed for the night.

Another ship lay in wait that night—a Belgian Relief ship called the *Imo*. She was meant to have left Halifax Harbour on December 5 but had been delayed by the late arrival of a coal tender. By the time the *Imo* had refuelled, it was too late for her to leave.

As fate would have it, the two ships found themselves heading directly towards each other on the morning of December 6. The *Imo,* having been forced to the Dartmouth side earlier that morning by another vessel, was in the wrong channel for outgoing ships. The *Mont Blanc* was in the right channel for incoming ships.

A number of signals were sounded—the *Mont Blanc* indicating that she was in the right, and the *Imo* responding that she was staying her course. At the same moment, both ships took decisive action, but it was too late to avoid a collision.

Almost at once, a spark created by the friction of the steel plates started a fire on the *Mont Blanc*. The crew and pilot took to the lifeboats and rowed furiously towards the Dartmouth shore, leaving the ship to drift towards Pier 6 in Richmond, a community in the North End of Halifax.

Little knowing that the burning ship was, in fact, a floating bomb, people rushed down to the harbour or to their windows to watch the spectacle. A few seconds before 9:05 A.M., the 3,000-ton *Mont Blanc* exploded.

Over 1,600 people were killed instantly, and hundreds more died in the hours and days that followed. The total is said to be close to 2,000, although the exact number will likely never be known. Nine thousand were injured. Hundreds of survivors suffered eye damage from flying glass, and many suffered permanent blindness. Twenty-five thousand people were left without adequate shelter and 6,000 were left homeless. The North End of Halifax—residential areas, factories, docks, and railway yards—was almost completely obliterated.

Many of the victims who weren't killed outright died in the tsunami that struck in the wake of the explosion, flooding in as high as eighteen metres above the high-water mark on the Halifax side. Others died in the fires caused by overturned stoves. Still others died trapped in the wreckage of their homes when word of another explosion forced everyone, including rescue workers, to flee the area. The rumour later turned out to be false.

The force was such that part of the *Mont Blanc*'s anchor shank, weighing over half a ton, landed three kilometres to the west of Halifax. Windows were shattered in homes a hundred kilometres away in Truro, Nova Scotia. The ground shook on Prince Edward Island, over three hundred kilometres away.

Relief efforts were quickly organized. Several thousand soldiers and sailors were in Halifax at the time, along with medical personnel, facilities, and supplies. Within three hours of the blast, City Hall officials had met with military commanders to organize transportation, food, and shelter. Rescue teams set to work at once, assisted by local volunteers.

Although some hospitals were performing operations within minutes of the explosion, they were scarcely able to cope with the enormous number of wounded. Camp Hill Hospital, built to accommodate 240 convalescing soldiers, was overwhelmed with some 1,400 victims.

Help from outside the city and province was soon on its way. By the end of the day, Canadian relief trains were arriving with surgeons, nurses, and medical supplies. Money poured in from all over the world. Assistance in the form of money, goods, and volunteers, not to mention trainloads of medical personnel and supplies, came from the people of Massachusetts. To this day, Halifax sends Boston an annual Christmas tree as an expression of gratitude.

The devastated area was rebuilt with astonishing speed, in spite of the harshness of the 1917/1918 winter. Within two months of the explosion, three thousand houses had been repaired and temporary apartments were being constructed at the rate of one per hour. Permanent housing in new developments would follow in the fall of 1918.

In early 1918, the Halifax Relief Commission was appointed to oversee the rebuilding of the North End and to provide compensation to victims for injuries and property loss. No amount of compensation, however, could make up for the lives that had been lost.

And the question remained: who was to blame for the disaster?

An inquiry known as the Wreck Commission began on December 13, 1917, exactly one week after the explosion. Over a month later, the *Mont Blanc*'s pilot, Francis Mackey, and French captain Aimé Le Medec were found to be wholly responsible for the collision and, ultimately, the explosion. Both men, along with the chief examining officer of the Royal Canadian Navy, were arrested on charges of manslaughter and criminal negligence. In March 1918, the charges were dismissed due to insufficient evidence. Captain Mackey, however, was unable to retrieve his pilot's license.

Over the course of several months and stretching into years, the owners of the *Imo* and the *Mont Blanc* filed for damages against each other. Decisions were appealed and counter-appealed. A decision in April 1918 before the Nova Scotia Admiralty Division of the Exchequer Court of Canada ruled entirely in favour of the *Imo.* In May 1919, the Supreme Court of Canada ruled that both ships were equally responsible and, consequently, neither was awarded damages.

The *Imo* then took the case to the highest judicial court at the time, the Privy Council of London, England. For five days in February 1920, this court heard evidence and arguments but ultimately focused on a crucial maritime law—both vessels had allowed themselves to get within 500 feet (152.4 metres) of each other. Everything that followed was a consequence of that one broken law. The *Imo* and the *Mont Blanc* were therefore equally to blame.

During the course of the civil suits, even after Mackey had been exonerated, the Federal Minister of Marine and Fisheries refused to reinstate him as an active pilot. No explanation was given. It wasn't until February 1922, after the defeat of the federal Conservative government, that Francis Mackey was reinstated as a pilot and able to resume piloting vessels in the Halifax Harbour. He did so until his retirement in 1937.

The Halifax Explosion has not been forgotten. Every year a memorial service is held to remember those whose lives were lost or shattered. It takes place on Fort Needham in Halifax's North End, beneath a massive memorial bell tower, every December 6 at 9:05 A.M. To this day, that fateful time remains permanently displayed on the north side clock of the City Hall Tower.

ACKNOWLEDGEMENTS

I am grateful to the many authors whose work I consulted in the writing of this book, particularly the following: Janet Kitz (*Shattered City*, *Survivors*, and *December 1917*), Janet Maybee (*The Persecution of Pilot Mackey* and *Aftershock*), and Laura M. MacDonald (*Curse of the Narrows*). Michelle Hébert Boyd's book *Enriched by Catastrophe: Social Work and Social Conflict after the Halifax Explosion* was immensely informative and helpful. I owe a debt of thanks to the staffs of the Maritime Museum of the Atlantic and the Nova Scotia Archives, whose assistance over many years of researching the Halifax Explosion have been invaluable.

My thanks to the friends and family who showed an interest in this project; to my husband Patrick for his endless patience and unfailing good humour, especially during the inevitable periods of frustration; and to my editor, Whitney Moran, whose chance remark triggered the idea that led to the book.